# CHILD'S PLAY
## *Cindi Myers*

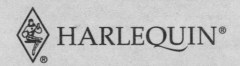
HARLEQUIN®

TORONTO • NEW YORK • LONDON
AMSTERDAM • PARIS • SYDNEY • HAMBURG
STOCKHOLM • ATHENS • TOKYO • MILAN • MADRID
PRAGUE • WARSAW • BUDAPEST • AUCKLAND

Recycling programs
for this product may
not exist in your area.

ISBN-13: 978-0-373-71549-7
ISBN-10:    0-373-71549-8

CHILD'S PLAY

Copyright © 2009 by Cynthia Myers.

www.eHarlequin.com

Printed in U.S.A.

## ABOUT THE AUTHOR

Cindi Myers was a monkey bars champ in elementary school, able to climb farther using only her arms than any boy on the playground. This did not, however, translate to any marketable skill as an adult, and she has since kept her feet planted firmly on the ground, allowing only her imagination to soar. She lives in the mountains of Colorado with her husband and two spoiled dogs.

### Books by Cindi Myers

**HARLEQUIN SUPERROMANCE**
1498—A SOLDIER COMES HOME
1530—A MAN TO RELY ON

**HARLEQUIN AMERICAN ROMANCE**
1182—MARRIAGE ON HER MIND
1199—THE RIGHT MR. WRONG

**HARLEQUIN NEXT**
MY BACKWARDS LIFE
THE BIRDMAN'S DAUGHTER

**HARLEQUIN ANTHOLOGY**
A WEDDING IN PARIS
  "Picture Perfect"

**HARLEQUIN SIGNATURE SELECT**
LEARNING CURVES
BOOTCAMP
  "Flirting with an Old Flame"

Don't miss any of our special offers. Write to us at the following address for information on our newest releases.

Harlequin Reader Service
U.S.: 3010 Walden Ave., P.O. Box 1325, Buffalo, NY 14269
Canadian: P.O. Box 609, Fort Erie, Ont. L2A 5X3

With much appreciation to Emily McKay,
for answering all my nosy questions
about pregnancy and newborns.
Any errors are mine alone.

# CHAPTER ONE

PEOPLE WHO TALKED about the excitement and glamour of business travel had obviously never done much of it.

Traveling alone was the worst, Diana thought, as she boarded the plane from New York to Denver. She hated slogging through airports by herself, spending endless hours sitting in uncomfortable chairs at the gates and knowing no one would be waiting for her at her destination. Then there were smaller annoyances, such as having to heft her own luggage into the overhead bin.

When she'd decided to buy that ceramic carousel music box at the baby boutique off Broadway, she hadn't considered how much heavier it would make the suitcase—and how impossible it would be for her seven-months-pregnant self to lift it.

"Let me help you with that."

A dark-haired man rose from his aisle seat. For a moment, their eyes locked and Diana caught her breath. He had eyes as blue as a Colorado sky, and she felt the impact of his gaze way down in her stomach—a giddy fluttering not unlike those first movements of the baby inside her.

The stranger easily lifted the suitcase into the bin, his

white oxford shirt stretching across his broad shoulders. Diana contemplated those shoulders, mentally measuring their width, imagining she knew exactly how the smooth cloth over taut muscle would feel beneath her hand.

The fantasy startled her. She almost laughed out loud at the absurdity of it. Even before her pregnancy, she had never been in the habit of lusting after strangers in airports or elsewhere. But even if she'd suddenly decided to develop a hitherto unexplored wild side, she couldn't imagine that her present condition would make her an object of desire for most men.

She realized the man was looking at her again, those blue eyes burning straight into hers with a hint of… anticipation? She had to glance away and attempt to regain her composure. "Thank you," she said, a bit breathlessly.

"Don't mention it." He started to sit again, and she glanced at her boarding pass to check her seat number. And had to choke back more surprised laughter. "I have the window seat," she said. "This one. Right by you." Did he think she was an idiot, babbling like this?

"No problem." He stepped back and allowed her to squeeze past.

Airplanes were definitely not made to accommodate bellies. And she wasn't even that big. Good thing this was her last flight until after the baby was born. She smoothed the tunic sweater over her abdomen a little self-consciously as she sat. Showing off a baby bump might be fashionable these days, but she still felt protective of herself. Not everyone reacted kindly to the lack of a ring on her finger.

She managed to shove her carry-on under the seat in front of her and buckle her seat belt, all the while concentrating on *not* staring at the man in the aisle seat. Amazingly enough, the seat between them stayed empty, a rare luxury these days. At least now she could indulge herself watching him out of the corner of her eye. As her mother always said, just because she wasn't interested in swimming in the ocean didn't mean she couldn't enjoy the view.

Once they were airborne, Diana reclined her seat slightly and eased her feet out of her low-heeled loafers. That was another side effect of pregnancy she hadn't anticipated—flying made her feet swell.

"Rough day?"

She glanced over and found him studying her, concern in his eyes. "Traveling is always tiring, I think," she said. She smoothed the tunic once more. "But especially now. This is my last trip before the baby is born."

"Ah. When are you due? That is…if you don't mind my asking."

The hesitancy behind his question charmed her. "Not at all," she said. "She's due in about eight weeks."

"A girl." He smiled. "I have a daughter."

"How old is she?"

"Kinsey is six." His smile vanished, replaced by a sadness so intense it made Diana's throat tighten. "She lives with her mother in Paris. I've just come from there. My first visit since they moved."

"That must be difficult for you, having her so far away."

He nodded, the muscles of his jaw working as if he was struggling to suppress strong emotion. "When I left her, she was crying. It was all I could do not to break down, too."

Diana wasn't used to men who were so open about their emotions. Her ex-husband Richard's idea of expressing his feelings was to thump his sons on the back or to swear more colorfully than usual. "I'm sure it means a lot to her, knowing you went all the way to Paris to see her," she said.

He nodded, though she suspected it was more out of politeness than out of any belief in the truth of her words. His obvious sorrow touched her, but after a moment, he visibly pulled himself together. "I'm Jason Benton," he said, offering his hand.

"Diana Shelton." His handshake was firm and warm. A thrill raced through her at the contact. Was her reaction only because she had been alone for the past few months or was there more going on here?

"Were you in New York on business or pleasure?" he asked.

"Business," she said. "Though I did manage to do some shopping, hence the extra-heavy suitcase."

"Do you live in Denver?"

She nodded. "And you?"

"In Evergreen. I'm superintendent of a Montessori school."

"I know exactly where that is." The town in the foothills of the Rocky Mountains was less than an hour's drive from her home in a Denver suburb. "I visited the school briefly several years ago, when I was first starting my business." She searched in her purse for a business card. "I design playscapes." Her designs had been built in schools, shopping centers, rec centers and parks in half a dozen states. Richard used to joke about his wife's job "playing with children." Of course, he hadn't objected to the money she brought in.

"Your children must love your job," Jason said. "Do they get to test all your designs?"

"Actually, this is my first child." She rested her hand on her bump.

He hid his surprise well. At forty, she knew she was older than most first-time mothers. "I have three step-children," she said. "Though they're all grown now."

"You and your husband must be excited about the new arrival," he said.

"Actually, we're divorced. It's a long story."

"I'm sorry."

She waited for him to add something about how brave she was—as if it took particular courage to do something when there was no other choice. Richard, who was fifteen years her senior and viewed the three children from his first marriage as burdens to be endured, had no desire to raise a fourth child at a time when he was contemplating retirement. He'd ordered her to choose between him and the baby she carried, and what little feeling she'd had left for him had died then and there.

"Divorce is never easy," she said. "But sometimes it's for the best." Every week, it seemed, she discovered new truths in that old cliché.

"Our divorce was my wife's idea, not mine," Jason said grimly. "But as you say, it was probably for the best. Except for our daughter."

"That is difficult," she said. "But I believe children are resilient." She hoped that was true, since her own child would grow up with a father who was distant, at best.

"Often more resilient than their parents," he said.

"What is your ex-wife doing in Paris?" she asked.

"Her new husband is from there. Candace is an artist. He's an actor." He shook his head. "Not the most settled environment for my daughter, but that's a whole other story."

A story Diana would have liked hearing, but she didn't want to press. She was enjoying their conversation too much to risk pushing him away. Whether it was fatigue or hormones or something mysterious in the cabin air, she felt a connection to this man she hadn't felt with anyone in, well, *years.*

"I won't bore you with all the details," he said. "I don't want to be one of those bitter ex-husbands who goes on and on to anyone who will listen about how he got the raw end of the deal. Tell me about your trip to New York. I haven't had the chance to spend much time in the city lately."

For the next hour, they talked—about New York, shopping, theater, books and movies. The conversation flowed easily from one subject to the next with the ease and intensity of old acquaintances catching up—or new friends eager to know everything about each other. Diana's fatigue vanished, replaced by the heady euphoria of attraction.

Even when they had to break off their conversation to accept the meager bags of pretzels and lukewarm cola that passed for refreshments, she was too aware of the man in the aisle seat. He'd spoken with such concern for his daughter—concern *her* child's father was apparently incapable of feeling.

Diana glanced at him again. Upon close inspection, she noted a hint of silver at his temples, and fine lines around his eyes that deepened when he smiled. At this hour of the afternoon his jaw showed the beginnings of a five-o'clock shadow, though he was otherwise impeccably groomed, from his neatly pressed shirt and pants to his fashionably cut hair and manicured nails.

He was definitely the kind of man who would catch any woman's eye—even one newly divorced and seven months pregnant. Add liking children enough to manage a school full of them, and being obviously devoted to his daughter to his list of qualities, and Jason Benton was definitely the kind of man she'd choose to star in her best fantasies.

OUT OF THE CORNER of his eye, Jason studied the woman in the window seat. Her light brown hair was drawn back from her face in a smooth chignon. Her skin was pale beneath a light dusting of makeup—he thought he could make out a few freckles. Her maternity top was made out of some expensive, silky material and her jewelry was chunky and ethnic looking.

The kind of thing Candace would have liked.

This reminder of his ex-wife darkened his mood. She'd received him coolly when he arrived at her Paris flat to pick up Kinsey. She'd greeted him at the door, barefoot and dressed in a Grecian-style gown, her auburn hair in wild disarray. She'd had a paintbrush stuck behind one ear and a streak of cadmium yellow across one cheek. "I'm in the middle of a commission and don't have time to talk," she'd said before he could utter one word.

He would have told her he had nothing to say to her, but Kinsey was standing there, her pink suitcase in her hand, her perfect heart-shaped face alight with antici-pation. So he'd turned his attention to her, ignoring both Candace and her new husband, Victor.

"Do you know what Candace's new husband said when I arrived to pick up my daughter?" he asked Diana when the flight attendant had moved on.

"What?" she asked. Her expression was attentive—interested. He welcomed the opportunity to sort out his muddled feelings by talking to her.

"He spoke French, and I'm not very fluent, but I'm sure he said something about the fact that I wore a suit to pick up Kinsey."

Her brow furrowed. "What's wrong with that?"

"Exactly what I was wondering. When Kinsey and I were alone in the taxi, I asked her if she thought my wearing a suit was odd. 'No,' she said. 'You always wear suits.' Then she said, 'Victor never wears a suit.'"

"Victor is your ex-wife's new husband?"

"Right. I couldn't decide if Kinsey thought the difference in the way we dressed was a good thing or a bad thing." What if she liked Victor's style better—thought he was friendlier, *cooler?* While her dad was just a stuffed shirt?

"I would think a child would see it as a good thing that the two of you are different," Diana said. "Victor has one role in her life, while you have another. Clearly different, with little ambiguity." She nodded. "Children like that, I think."

"Maybe so. Her mother and I are certainly different enough." His relationship with Candace had always been of the oil-and-water variety. She was artistic, impulsive, messy and irresponsible. He was neat, ordered and methodical. He'd seen them as a case of opposites attracting, each of them filling in the blank spaces of the other.

"I used to think the difference between us would make our marriage stronger," he said. "I told myself our problems were just the ordinary rough spots any marriage had to weather. Now I see how naive I was."

"I know exactly what you mean," Diana said. "I thought Richard and I were happy, too. Only after we'd separated did I realize I'd mistaken complacency for contentment."

Was that what he'd been—*complacent?* "Most of the time Candace and I *were* happy," he said. "Or at least *I* was. And Kinsey was, too." He smiled, remembering the first time he'd held his daughter. "She was the most beautiful baby. I fell in love with her the first moment her blue eyes looked into mine."

"She's a very lucky little girl," Diana said, her voice wistful. "Richard was never close to his children. I told myself it was because he's very reserved. Now I think it's more that he's too selfish to want to put forth the effort to build relationships with others."

Jason felt a stab of sympathy for the man. Keeping a little distance between oneself and others would probably prevent a lot of pain. All the happiness he'd known had crumbled like a sugar castle the afternoon Candace told him she was leaving, and taking Kinsey with her. He'd struggled through the divorce and the contentious custody arrangements, too shell-shocked to protest when their lawyers and the judge decided that seeing his daughter every other weekend was enough.

It clearly wasn't enough, but Candace had been good about allowing him ample access to Kinsey. All he'd ever wanted was to care for and protect his family. The failure haunted him, but he did his best to adjust. Then Candace had announced she was not only remarrying, but her new husband was a Frenchman, a native of Paris. They would be relocating to a flat on the Left Bank, and taking Kinsey with them.

He'd tried to fight her decision, but couldn't even get a court date before she was gone.

He glanced at Diana once more, at the gentle swelling of her abdomen beneath her tunic. How could a man divorce a woman who carried his unborn child?

Then again, maybe *she'd* divorced *him*. Maybe he was involved with someone else. Or *she* had a lover.

"Of course, it wasn't too long after Candace told me she wanted a divorce that I realized she had someone else," he said. "I don't know if it was Victor, or if he showed up later. I don't really care. I only care about what our divorce means for Kinsey."

"Having her so far away isn't ideal, of course," Diana said. "But you're making it work. You're doing your best, and I think children know these things."

He nodded, glum. "This visit was really tough," he said. "Every happy minute felt tainted by the knowledge that I'd be leaving soon. I did my best to hide my feelings from Kinsey, but I'm afraid she sensed my sadness. She hugged me more often, and told me over and over how much she loved me, as if she was trying to reassure me." Kinsey had stood on the curb and waved as his taxi pulled away, tears streaming down her face. He'd known then why parents sometimes kidnapped their own children. He'd never felt so helpless and desperate in his life. He swallowed past a painful tightness in his throat, and blinked back stinging tears.

"I'm sure she does love you. Very much," Diana said softly. She reached out and touched his arm, briefly, but the gesture of comfort cut through his sorrow, if only for a moment.

"I'm thinking of trying to get custody of my daughter." He wasn't the type to divulge such personal information to a stranger, but Diana no longer felt like a stranger. He sensed he could tell her almost anything and she'd understand—which was wild, considering how utterly uninterested he'd been in any woman since his divorce. Who would have thought his libido would suddenly wake up at 30,000 feet? And with a woman who was seven months pregnant?

"Oh?" Her finely arched eyebrows drew together in a frown. "Did something happen in Paris? Something to make you concerned for your daughter?"

"Only that I know she'd be happier back in Colorado with me, living in the house she grew up in, going to the same school, with the same friends. My ex lives a rather…Bohemian lifestyle."

Diana's lips quirked up in the hint of a smile, dimples forming on either side of her mouth. "I have to admit, when I was your daughter's age, I'd have been thrilled at the chance to live in Paris. I thought growing up in small-town Iowa was the most boring thing in the world."

"Kinsey was excited at first, but now she really misses Colorado." And she missed *him*. That knowledge intensified the hurt in his chest.

"Then I wish you luck," Diana said. "It's not an easy situation, no matter what happens."

The pilot announced they would be landing soon. "Good luck to you, too," Jason said. He fingered the business card he'd stuck into his pocket. Was it only because he was feeling so at sea emotionally that he felt such a connection with her? Their brief conversation had been among the most pleasant he'd enjoyed in months. "Maybe…could I call you sometime?" he asked. "To see how you're doing?"

She hesitated, then nodded. "Yes…I'd like that."

"Then I will." He certainly hadn't boarded this flight with romance on his mind, but that only proved how unpredictable life could be. He'd never have thought he'd be a single father at this point in his life, either. For too long, he'd let his divorce stop him in his tracks. Candace had clearly moved on with her life; it was time he moved on, as well.

DIANA LET HERSELF into the house she was renting on a quiet side street in Lakewood, a suburb on the southwest side of Denver. The lovely Craftsman-style house had only two bedrooms and one bath, which made it cheaper to rent and perfect for her needs. Beautiful hardwood floors, large windows that let in plenty of southern light, and a mature flower garden out back had sealed the deal. She'd turned the second bedroom into a nursery and claimed the small formal dining room as her office.

She parked her suitcase and computer bag beside the kitchen counter, gathered the pile of mail that had collected in front of the slot in the door, and pressed the play button on the answering machine.

"Hi, Di. Hope your trip to New York went well." The voice of her youngest stepson, Steve, filled the room. "Eric and I wondered if you'd like to have dinner with us Wednesday night. Call me."

She made a note on the pad by the phone to call Steve and accept the invitation. His partner, Eric, was a successful architect and fabulous cook, and the two were always fun to visit with.

The next three calls were from clients with questions about bids or projects in various stages of completion.

The last call began with a woman's strident voice. "I can't believe you're flying across the country in your condition. I'm sure it can't be good for you. Or the baby."

"And I can't believe you're so concerned about me or the baby," Diana said out loud. She and Richard's youngest child had been at odds since the first time they were introduced. Claire had feared Diana was taking her place as number one in her father's affections, and had fought back with every weapon at her disposal ever since. Since Claire could do no wrong in Richard's eyes, Diana had learned to ignore the girl's tantrums and manipulations.

"I need you to look after Baxter while Derek and I are in Saint Lucia for a week," Claire continued. "The resort we're visiting was highly recommended by my friend Patricia. She was pregnant by the time she and her husband returned from their babymoon there. Call me and I'll give you the dates. You should be available, right? I mean, I hope you're not planning more travel this close to your due date."

Diana dutifully noted the call on her notepad, then drew a small frowny face next to it. Baxter was Claire's miniature schnauzer. He was a sweet dog whom Diana feared was in for a rude awakening if and when Claire succeeded with her plans to conceive a child. So far, Claire's efforts had been for naught, but not, Diana gathered, for want of trying. The "babymoon" to Saint Lucia was apparently her latest approach to the problem.

A problem that hadn't even existed until Diana herself had become pregnant.

The baby kicked. Diana smiled and rubbed her belly, anticipating the day when she'd caress her child. *How many years I waited for you to arrive,* she'd tell her.

Now she blamed herself for waiting so long.

Richard had told her early in their relationship that he didn't want more children. At first, she'd believed this didn't matter—that being with him was enough for her. Later, she'd convinced herself she could change his mind. But he was clearly horrified at the idea, pointing to difficulties with the three children he already had.

Diana agreed that Steve, Marcus and particularly Claire had not been easy children, though Richard's indifference to the boys and catering to Claire were surely partly to blame.

Diana hadn't pressed the issue. She'd tried to fill her need to be around children by volunteering with an inner-city parks program. That had led to working on plans for a playground and eventually the establishment of her own business designing playscapes.

Her success had been bittersweet, exposing her to more and more children—none of them her own.

When she'd first missed her period late last year she'd chalked it up to a stressful schedule and what she thought was a lingering flu. When her doctor had delivered the news that she was pregnant, she'd been stunned. She was almost home from seeing him when the impact of his words hit her, and she had pulled the car to the side of the road and wept for joy.

She'd greeted Richard at the door that evening, anxious to share the news, sure he'd be happy once his initial shock wore off. After all, his children were all grown now. Most of his friends already had grandchildren. Wouldn't the idea of having a son or daughter with *her* please him?

He had been anything but pleased. He'd accused her of deliberately conceiving in order to thwart him. Declaring he wouldn't be trapped, he'd walked out. By the next day, he'd calmed down, but made it very clear she would have to choose between the baby and him.

Claire had even weighed in, accusing Diana of deliberately conceiving in order to embarrass *her.* Like her father, Claire viewed everything through the lens of how it affected her.

Diana went into the bedroom and unpacked, carefully retrieving the carousel music box. She carried it into the nursery, which months ago she'd painted in a soft green with lavender trim. Colors, Claire had informed her, that were totally unsuitable for a newborn.

Diana wound the box and set it atop the dresser. The carousel began to turn and a tinkly version of "When You Wish Upon a Star" filled the room. She would play this every night, to help lull her daughter to sleep.

Only a few short weeks until her due date, and she still had so much to do. She had to buy a car seat and see about birthing classes. What with the divorce and moving into her own place, the months had flown by.

At first, she'd been devastated by Richard's rejection of her and her child. But she'd passed quickly into anger, then into a feeling it had taken her a while to identify as relief. She hadn't realized how stressful living with Richard hâd been until she was on her own.

Yes, she was sad that something that had begun so wonderfully had ended, and that her daughter might never know the love of a truly good father. But that sadness was eased by Diana's excitement over finally being able to live life as she wanted.

She returned to her bedroom and continued to unpack, thinking of the man she'd met on the plane, Jason. A thrill shimmered through her. She couldn't remember ever being so strongly attracted to a man. Even in the early days of their relationship she'd experienced more awe and respect for Richard than this…this physical *connection* to a person. It was wild.

In addition to being gorgeous, Jason was a genuinely nice guy. And a good father. Her maternal instincts had obviously been drawn to that side of him. He had been so clearly heartbroken over leaving his daughter. What kind of woman would divorce a man like that?

Maybe he had another side to him she didn't know about. Maybe he was a philanderer, or was emotionally distant or cruel.

He'd said he'd call her. Part of her thought the last thing she needed right now was a man in her life. But surely a phone call wouldn't hurt. Maybe a coffee date. Just to test the waters, so to speak.

But no rushing into anything serious. In all those

years of deferring to Richard she'd forgotten how wonderful independence could be. The divorce had shook her out of a complacent daze she'd been in for far too long. Now, decisions as simple as choosing a paint color for the nursery walls or what to have for dinner delighted her. She was reluctant for anyone—no matter how handsome or charming—to intrude upon this new romance with herself.

# CHAPTER TWO

AFTER THE QUIET of his empty house, Jason welcomed the noise and energy of the Evergreen Montessori School. As he crossed the playground Monday morning, taking a shortcut from the parking lot to his office, students greeted him from the swings and slides. "Hello, Mr. Benton!" called a curly haired first-grader.

"Hi, Mr. B.," said a third-grade boy who dangled upside down from the jungle gym.

"Hello, Violet. Careful there, Henry." He nodded hello to the other students, and to Mrs. Parks, the teacher on playground duty this morning.

Inside, he breathed in the familiar school scents of floor polish and dusty tennis shoes. He paused to check the bulletin board near the entrance, and straightened a notice of an upcoming bake sale sponsored by the school choir to fund their participation in a summer City Concert series.

The library occupied an open pod at the center of the building. It was empty at this time of day, but Jason stopped to neatly stack a few books that had been left scattered among the beanbag chairs in the reading area.

"Good morning, Jason. How was your trip to Paris?"

His best friend, instructor Graham Sparks, leaned out of his classroom.

"Kinsey and I had a great visit," he said. "She must have grown two inches since I saw her last." The thought pained him; how many other events in her life would happen without him there?

Graham, the father of six children, thumped Jason on the shoulder. "You'll see her again before you know it," he said. "And I've been thinking. Why don't we set up a webcam at your house, and send one to her, as well? You could see each other while you're talking."

"That's a great idea," Jason said. Though he hoped not to need that sort of thing to keep in touch with his daughter much longer. His goal was to have her with him permanently by the time the school year ended.

"I'll research equipment and we can talk later," Graham said.

"Thanks." Jason continued to his office at the back of the school. The original design had called for the office at the front entrance, as was usual for schools, but he liked the idea of having to walk through the space to reach his private area. It allowed him to keep tabs on all the goings-on each day. Plus the arrangement physically put the focus on the kids, and their learning, while the administration remained secondary.

"Mr. Reisler is on the line," his secretary, Evie, told him.

"Thanks." Jason walked into his office and picked up the phone. "Hello, Scott," he said to the friend and lawyer who had seen him through the divorce.

"I got your message," Scott said without preamble. "About wanting to sue for custody of your daughter. I think it's a bad idea."

Jason lowered himself into the high-backed leather desk chair. "Why do you say that? I just spent a week with Kinsey in Paris and I know she'd be happy living here with me."

"Is she *unhappy* over there with her mother and stepfather?"

Jason frowned at this reference to Victor as Kinsey's stepfather. The man would never be a father of any kind to his daughter. Still, Kinsey had seemed content enough, and had chatted about her school and the friends she'd made. But she'd also talked about how much she missed her home in Colorado. "She'd be happier with me," he said.

He thought Scott let out a heavy sigh. "Look, Jason, I'm going to be blunt here. No one wins in these battles. You want her because you love her, but Candace loves her, too. There's no real reason to change the custody agreement. To a judge, it's going to look like you're doing this solely to make trouble for your ex-wife."

"I'm doing this because I love my daughter and I believe she would be better off living with me than thousands of miles away with Candace and a man who's a stranger to her."

"He's hardly a stranger. Candace and he have been married, what, three months now?"

Jason took a deep breath, trying to remain calm. "Taking Kinsey away from all her friends and family, from the only home she's ever known, was wrong," he said. "It's the kind of irresponsible, impulsive behavior Candace has always been prone to." Once, when they were still married, Candace had decided to trade in her minivan, which she had chosen only two years before, for a sports car. The low-slung convertible was impractical in their mountain climate, and Kinsey's car seat would barely fit in it. When Jason had pointed this out, Candace had shrugged and said she could borrow his Jeep whenever she wanted to, so why not have at least one vehicle that was fun?

"Living with me, Kinsey would be in a familiar environment, with people she knows and loves, and a stable routine," he concluded.

"Is Candace neglecting Kinsey?"

He hesitated. "No, of course not. But the child has no schedule. She doesn't even have a regular bedtime. I asked her what she ate for dinner the night before I picked her up and she said Victor had served *pan au chocolate* because Candace was working on a commission."

"French pastry every once in a while isn't going to hurt any child," Scott said. "And not to bring up a sore point, but I seem to recall that Candace's spontaneity, creativity and dedication to her work were all things you admired about her."

Jason winced. Yes, when he'd first met Candace, he'd been impressed by her ability to cast aside worries and enjoy the moment. As someone with a constant to-do list in his head, such freedom and abandon had been as exotic and appealing as a trip down the Nile. But what had seemed fun and adventurous when they were dating became a nightmare of unpaid bills and missed appointments in their early marriage. He'd solved the problem by taking charge of their finances and leaving her reminders about important dates. Instead of being grateful for his help, though, she'd called him controlling and obsessive.

"That was all fine when she didn't have a child to look after," he said. "She's thirty-five years old. It's time she grew up." He pinched the top of his nose, trying to ward off a headache. "Whose side are you on, anyway?"

"Believe it or not, yours. I don't think it's healthy for you to obsess about this."

He was not *obsessing*. Or at least, not any more than any father who'd had his daughter taken from him. "If you don't want to take the case, I'll hire someone else," he said.

"No, if you're going to insist on doing this, I'll represent you. And I'll do my best for you. But be prepared for a hard fight."

"Where my daughter is concerned, nothing is too hard."

"Come into my office tomorrow about four and I'll have some papers for you to sign."

Jason hung up the phone and almost immediately the intercom on his desk buzzed. "Mrs. Polis is here to see you," Evie said.

Beverly Polis was the attractive single mother of two sweet, smart children who attended the school. An accountant who operated a business out of her home, she also headed up the school's parent booster club and served on the board of directors.

"I hope I'm not interrupting anything," she said as she entered the office. Petite, with a cap of short, dark hair and expressive brown eyes, she wore tailored pants and a silk blouse that were obviously expensive but not ostentatious. Jason had heard that her ex-husband was a wealthy surgeon whom she'd caught having an affair with his office manager. He paid the bills for the children's schooling.

"I'm never too busy to talk to you," Jason said cheerfully. After his less-than-satisfactory conversation with Scott, he welcomed the opportunity to focus his thoughts elsewhere. "Please, sit down and tell me how I can help you."

"I have some good news," she said. She removed a file folder from her leather tote and opened it on the desk. "The boosters met yesterday and voted to use the money we raised from the fall carnival and the holiday bazaar to build a new playground for the school."

Jason sat back in his chair. "What's wrong with the playground we have?" he asked. True, it had been built when the school was first constructed, which made it ten years old, but he saw to it that it was well-maintained, and the children seemed to enjoy it.

The faintest lines creased Beverly's forehead. "It's very old-fashioned and utilitarian," she said. "We want something more innovative, something to encourage children's imaginations."

"Not plastic," he said, picturing the garish playscape Kinsey had insisted they spend time exploring in a McDonald's off the Champs-Élysées.

"Oh, no, not plastic!" Beverly was clearly horrified by this idea. "We have the name of a designer who's been recommended. She works in natural materials and does some really innovative things."

He glanced at the business card she handed him and his heart did a stutter-step. *Child's Play Designs, by Diana Shelton.* He had an identical card in his wallet, tucked behind Kinsey's phone number.

"Is something wrong?" Beverly leaned toward him. "You're very quiet all of a sudden."

"No, nothing's wrong." He laid the card on the desk. "Actually, I've met Ms. Shelton."

"That's wonderful. I was hoping you'd agree to contact her about designing a playscape for the school." She laughed. "They don't even call them playgrounds anymore."

He nodded, still distracted by thoughts of the woman he'd met on the plane. Diana Shelton had been on his mind off and on since they'd parted. Her pregnancy had made her seem vulnerable, yet she'd radiated a quiet strength. He'd been planning to call her when the time seemed right. He didn't want to rush into anything. Was Beverly's mention of her merely an odd coincidence, or some kind of cosmic nudge?

"Call me after you've talked to Ms. Shelton," Beverly said. "Maybe we can have lunch and discuss her suggestions."

Her eyes met his. He wondered if she was flirting. For the first time, he considered her as more than merely the parent of two of his students. She was attractive, smart and organized—exactly the sort of woman who should appeal to him. Yet he felt nothing beyond a pleasant friendship for her. No heightened awareness or sharp edge of desire that signaled the possibility of a more intense relationship.

None of the feelings he'd experienced during that magical few hours on the plane with Diana.

"I'll give Ms. Shelton a call," he said, escorting Beverly to the door. He was curious to know if his attraction to her would be as strong after a second meeting.

WHEN DIANA PULLED INTO the parking lot of Evergreen Montessori School two days later, she paused for a moment to smooth her hair and reapply a coat of pink lipstick. She'd been surprised, and pleased, to hear from Jason, the pleasure dampened only slightly by the knowledge that he was contacting her for business reasons. Of course, she always welcomed new clients, but the female part of her—the part that currently felt dumpy and awkward and anything but sexy—had momentarily rejoiced that, even in her present condition, a handsome man like Jason might have found her attractive enough to pursue.

Not, of course, that she was interested in a relationship. But ego had little to do with logic sometimes. She collected her briefcase and followed the concrete walkway to the front entrance. A guard at the door checked her ID and issued her a name badge, then directed her to the administrative offices at the rear of the building.

The school was an open, airy space, filled with light from windows and skylights. The hallways were painted pale yellow with orange trim. Low walls in the center of the building sectioned off a library with comfortable chairs and colorful beanbags scattered between the shelves.

A small sign directed her to the offices, where a pleasant-faced woman greeted her. "You must be Ms. Shelton. I'll tell Mr. Benton you're here."

The Jason Benton who greeted her was a more energetic, upbeat version of the travel-weary man she'd encountered on the plane. His smile sent a serious heat wave through her, and when he clasped her hand, she had to resist holding on a little longer than was absolutely necessary. "How have you been?" he asked. "You're looking well."

"I've been great. You're looking good yourself." Very good. He wore a blue dress shirt that emphasized his eyes, and a blue-and-silver tie and dark gray pants. He also smelled good—like an expensive, spicy cologne. He must have women lining up outside his office with excuses as to why they had to see him.

"Why don't we start with a tour of the school and the existing playground," he said.

"I'd love that."

He escorted her from the office. "We refer to this as

the equivalent of our refrigerator door," he said, indicating a large section of wall covered with students' artwork. "We rotate the pieces weekly, so that every student gets a chance to show off his or her work," he explained.

He held a door for her and they entered a small, pleasant lunchroom. Instead of long cafeteria tables, students were seated at smaller, round tables. Classical music provided a counterpoint to the low hum of conversation. "Hi, Sheila," Jason said to the woman at the cash register. "What's on the menu today?"

"It's pizza day, Mr. B."

"Homemade pizza," Jason said to Diana. "We have pepperoni and vegetarian, with a whole-wheat crust and low-fat cheese."

"The kids love it," Sheila said. "So do the teachers and administrators." She pointed a thumb at Jason.

He laughed. "I'll admit I eat more than my share."

Not that Diana could tell. He was trim and fit. They returned to the hallway.

"Are you familiar with the Montessori Method?" he asked.

"Not really," Diana admitted. "I gather it has something to do with encouraging children to learn at their own pace?"

"That's part of it. Dr. Maria Montessori believed children learned best when encouraged to follow their natural proclivities for exploring and discovering." He opened another door and led her into an empty classroom. It was decorated with posters and more student artwork, and furnished with low tables and comfortable chairs in addition to student desks. "Unlike traditional classrooms, our school is set up with learning centers that children are free to explore as they are led," Jason said. He had a pleasant speaking voice, low-pitched and soothing. Richard, on the other hand, had spoken every sentence as if he was giving an order.

"While a classroom may have thirty students, the children work mostly independently," Jason continued. "The teachers instruct individually and in small groups, and students remain with the same teacher and most of the same classmates for three years."

"So you'll want your playscape to reflect this same philosophy of encouraging students to explore and learn," she said.

He glanced at her, a hint of amusement in his brilliant blue eyes. "I've always thought of playground equipment's primary function as being to allow children to let off steam and have fun."

She laughed. "Of course it's designed so they'll have fun. But it can also encourage them to use their imaginations and to explore the world around them." *Her* imagination was working overtime at the moment, creating scenarios where the two of them could spend extended periods of time alone. That she could feel this way about *anyone* after her ordeal with Richard both surprised and delighted her.

They exited onto the existing playground. It was fairly typical of older configurations—a swing set, a slide, a set of monkey bars and a roundabout, all placed on beds of sand and cedar chips. About a dozen children ran and played in the area, overseen by a woman with the perpetually worried expression of someone who would prefer to be sitting somewhere quiet with a cup of tea and a good book. Adjacent to the playground was a soccer field and basketball court, both empty.

"I'm sure the children have a lot of fun on this equipment," Diana said. Experience had taught her not to be too critical of a facility's current setup. People tended to feel proprietary and sometimes defensive.

"How do you think we could improve it?" Jason asked.

"Often, I design around a theme," she said. "I've done playscapes built as Western forts, with climbing walls and tepees and swings shaped like horses. I've done a pirate ship and a castle and a space station. And I once did a fantasy-scape with swings like sea horses, a treasure cave and giant books."

"We don't want anything too out-there," Jason said. "And nothing too garish."

She studied the wood and natural stone of the building's exterior and the snow-capped mountain peaks rising in the distance. "You're right," she said. "We should do something in keeping with the natural setting." She turned to him. "I'll need to get some more information before I draw up my ideas—enrollment, budget, things like that."

"Of course." He checked his watch and she felt her spirits sink. He was probably going to tell her he'd have to get back to her later. She'd enjoyed talking with him so much she hated for their time together to end.

"It's almost lunchtime," he said. "Why don't we eat

and discuss this further? There's a good café not far from here. Unless you'd rather have pizza?"

"The café sounds great." She felt almost giddy at the prospect and told herself to calm down. After all, Jason was a client and this was strictly a business relationship.

At least it was so far.

DIANA HAD FORGOTTEN the pleasure of enjoying a meal while seated across from a handsome man who appeared interested in everything she had to say. The conversation wasn't earthshaking; they discussed the particulars of the job, such as budget, number of students who would be using the playscape and things like that. But Jason's attention, his warm smile and intelligent comments were a decided boost to her ego.

And that surprising physical connection to him that she'd felt on the plane still charged the air around them and provided additional meaning for every look or brush of a hand.

She was reminded of those early days in her relationship with Richard, when their encounters had been charged with a heightened awareness of every gesture he made, or inflection of his voice. Every conversation had a subtext of sensuality.

Of course, she'd been a different woman then, naive enough to be impressed that a distinguished professor fifteen years her senior would take an interest in her, a lowly first-year grad student. In those days, she'd admired his forceful manner, mistaking it as a sign of masculine power. She'd seen his strong opinions as the mark of a man who had experienced the world and had gained the insight and maturity necessary to judge it.

Only later had she recognized the immaturity behind his insistence on always having his own way.

"How did you get involved in designing playscapes?" Jason asked. "It seems a very specialized field."

"My undergraduate degree is in art and design. Then I decided I wanted to teach, so I was working on a masters in education when I married and quit school. My husband was one of my professors and he thought it would look bad for him to marry a student, so he persuaded me to drop out before our wedding." The surge of old anger at that long-ago concession surprised her a little. Then again, a lot of past hurts had resurfaced since the divorce, things she'd successfully suppressed for decades suddenly demanding to be acknowledged.

"But how did you end up designing playscapes?" Jason asked.

"I'm sorry, I didn't really answer your question, did I? I didn't work at all the first ten years I was married. My husband was older and didn't want me working. His children spent every other weekend and summers with us, but that really wasn't enough to keep me busy, so I started volunteering. I did all the usual things—women's shelter, the art museum, the library. Then I got involved with a program designed to enrich the lives of inner-city children. At first I taught art, then I was on a committee tasked with building a park at a housing project. There was a competition to design the playscape and I submitted a proposal under my maiden name. To my astonishment, I won." She smiled, the joy of that moment still alive within her. "There was a small newspaper article, then a magazine story about the completed park. I began getting calls, asking me to design for parks, rec centers, schools and hospitals."

"What did your husband think of your sudden success?"

"He was supportive as long as it didn't inconvenience him. He didn't like me traveling, and complained whenever my work interfered with his plans." She frowned. "I think what bothered him most of all was that I was doing things outside of his sphere of influence. He couldn't control me anymore. And of course, I think he resented having to share the spotlight with me at parties and in the local news."

"Well, you came highly recommended to us."

She would have thought she was past the age when a man's smile could make her heart flutter, but obviously she wasn't. "I've been limiting the new projects I take on as it gets closer to my delivery date," she said. "But I'm confident I can complete your drawings before then. If you approve the project, we can start construction after my maternity leave."

"When is your due date?"

"June 6, though I understand with first babies I could deliver early or late."

"My daughter was a week late. My wife was beside herself with anxiety. I was, too."

"Have you spoken with your daughter since your return home?"

"Yes. I called to tell her I'd made it back safely."

"Do you have a picture? I'd love to see her."

He took out his wallet and opened it to a photo of a smiling blond girl with eyes the same sapphire shade as his. "She's adorable," Diana said.

"I think so." He replaced the wallet. "Then again, I might be a little prejudiced." His expression sobered. "I talked to my lawyer about suing for custody."

"Oh." She wasn't sure what to say. She understood he missed his daughter terribly, but as a woman about to be a mother herself, she felt a sharp sympathy for his ex-wife also. "What did he say?"

"He's against it. But I'm determined. My ex-wife isn't a bad person. I know she loves Kinsey, and Kinsey loves her. But Candace is an artist. She leads a very… erratic life. There's no structure, and while I don't think children should be regimented, they need some kind of dependable schedule. Candace can be very immature and irresponsible."

All the happy fantasies featuring Jason that Diana had allowed herself to indulge in vaporized with his words. She had once overheard Richard describe *her* almost the same way—immature, irresponsible and, perhaps most damning of all in his eyes, an artist.

While she found Jason's concern for his daughter touching, she fought the urge to defend his ex. After all, since her divorce she'd enjoyed living her own unstructured life, exploring new ideas and activities and trying to discover parts of her personality she'd suppressed in her years of marriage.

"Then, of course, there's Victor. He's a French actor, so his lifestyle is even more erratic than Candace's. He's never had children before, and he admitted to me that he'd never even been around them much before he met Candace. I can't think he's going to be much of a stepfather to Kinsey."

Diana heard the resentment underlying these sentences, and chose her next words carefully. "When Richard and I married, I'd never had children, either. I was only twenty-two and suddenly I had three children I was responsible for, at least part of the time. Claire was eight and the boys were eleven and twelve. I'm sure his ex-wife thought I would be a horrible influence."

Jason had the grace to look sheepish. "I'll admit I don't like the man. I resent him being with my daughter when I can't be. That may have colored my judgment of him."

His contrition tempered her disappointment. Jason wasn't Richard—though they were both men, with a man's desire to remain in *control*. "You're in a tough position," she agreed. "I know in my case, it was frustrating for all of us. Even though Richard had been divorced two years before he and I started dating, I was much younger than him or his ex, and unsure of myself. I really didn't have the authority to discipline the kids and they took advantage of that, at least at first. Richard wasn't good about backing me up, and I felt their mother tried to thwart me at every turn." She shook her head, remembering those turbulent days. "I'm looking forward to raising my daughter without so many outside opinions. In fact, it's been nice living my *life* without someone else trying to dictate my choices."

"Candace accused me of being a control freak before she left," he said, avoiding Diana's gaze. "I'd suggested we make it a point to have dinner as a family at a specific time each weeknight."

The idea itself wasn't controlling, but she knew from experience that sometimes the words that were said didn't matter as much as *how* they were said. And who knew how many other such proclamations he'd made? Maybe, as with Diana herself, Jason's ex had eventually found the weight of all such dictates to be too heavy.

"Diana! What are you doing here?"

They both turned toward the slim young woman who spoke, and Diana inwardly winced as her stepdaughter, Claire, strode toward them.

## CHAPTER THREE

CLAIRE HAD OBVIOUSLY come from the gym, her pink velour workout suit coordinating with her pink leather tennis shoes and pink water bottle. Her long brown hair was pulled up in a high ponytail and a pair of sunglasses perched atop her head. She looked beautiful, healthy and—as usual when she was around Diana— peeved.

"Did you get my message about Baxter?" she asked, stopping beside their table.

"Jason, this is Claire Fitzsimmons. Claire, this is Jason Benton." Diana made the introductions. "Jason is the superintendent of the Evergreen Montessori School. Claire is my stepdaughter."

Claire wrinkled her nose. She hated being reminded of their relationship, even though Diana had been a part of her life since the girl was eight. She nodded stiffly to Jason, then returned her attention to Claire. "Did you get my message about Baxter?" she asked once more.

"Yes, but you didn't say what dates you'd be out of town."

"May 18th through the 25th," she said. "We're going to Saint Lucia," she added for Jason's benefit.

"I'll have to check my calendar and get back to you," Diana said.

"Why do you need to check your calendar?" Claire's voice rose in exasperation. "Surely you aren't planning on traveling anywhere in *your* condition."

Diana let the comment go unanswered; the best way to thwart Claire was to refuse to argue with her. "I'll call you," she said. "If you'll excuse me…"

"Would you like to join us?" Jason asked. He stood, one hand on the back of a chair as if to pull it out for Claire.

Diana wished he wasn't quite such a gentleman. The last thing she wanted was for Claire to intrude on what had been, until now, a very nice lunch.

"No, thank you. I have an appointment to get my nails done. I just stopped in to grab a salad." Claire frowned at the remains of the grilled tilapia on Diana's plate. "I've read that pregnant women shouldn't eat fish. Aren't you worried about mercury levels damaging the baby?"

Diana gritted her teeth. Claire wasn't the only person who felt free to dispense unwanted advice about pregnancy, simply the most annoying of the self-styled pregnancy police. "My doctor assured me that farm-raised tilapia is perfectly safe."

Claire sniffed. "Well, *I* certainly wouldn't take any chances." Then she turned and walked to the café's front counter to place her order.

Jason waited until Claire had left the restaurant before he spoke. "So that's your stepdaughter."

"That's her." Diana poked at the rice pilaf beside her

fish. "I have a good relationship with Marcus and Steve, Claire's brothers. But she and I have never really gotten along, though I try to keep peace between us for the sake of the rest of the family." She didn't want the boys to have to choose between her and their only sister.

"I guess divorce is tough on everyone involved," he said.

"I'm no expert, but I think Claire's behavior was created by more than the divorce," Diana said. "Her father spoiled her terribly, then would completely ignore her when he felt like it. So she was always competing for his attention. That could warp anybody."

"Still, I've seen how divorce affects children in my school. Some of them act out, while others try to be supernaturally good. It makes me worry about Kinsey even more."

He was looking miserable again, and Diana's heart ached for him. She touched the back of his hand. "You sound like a great dad to me," she said. "And I'm sure Kinsey knows that."

He looked down at her hand atop his, and Diana felt again the zing of attraction. When his eyes met hers they held a heat that hadn't been there before. She quickly withdrew her hand and sat back, suddenly breathless. Time to slow things down.

He must have felt the same way, because he busied himself studying their bill. "Let me get this," he said, taking out his credit card. "When do you think you could have some drawings and ideas to me?"

"Would next week be soon enough?"

"That would be great."

They parted in the school parking lot and exchanged cordial goodbyes. Diana watched him in her rearview mirror as he crossed the lot toward the school entrance. He walked with his hands in his pockets, his head down, as if deep in thought. Was she vain to wonder if he was thinking about her?

More likely, his thoughts were on his daughter. No doubt the fact that he no longer had the control over his daughter's life that he'd once enjoyed was making their separation that much harder on him. Diana sympathized with his desire to have her with him, but his remarks about his ex-wife, the irresponsible artist, still stung. Jason wasn't bombastic and narcissistic like Richard, but he was definitely a man who liked things to be done a certain way. And hadn't she had enough of that the past eighteen years?

HIS LUNCH WITH DIANA left Jason with mixed feelings. On one hand, he was fascinated by this intelligent woman who, while clearly the creative type, was also down-to-earth and responsible. Yet her comments about her stepchildren and her insistence on raising her child her own way reminded him too much of the many arguments he had had with Candace over the proper approach to rearing Kinsey.

"A long lunch with a pretty woman. I'd say things are looking up for you." Graham found Jason in the men's washroom, drying his hands.

"What do you know about it?" Jason asked.

"Evie was quick to spread the news in the staff lunchroom." Graham leaned against the door, blocking Jason's exit. "So tell me about her. Evie says she's pregnant. Not yours, I take it."

"No!" He flushed, then realized Graham was giving him a hard time. "Did Evie also mention the woman is designing a new playscape for the school? We had lunch to discuss the particulars."

"What's her name?"

"Diana Shelton."

"Is she single?"

"Yes. Divorced."

"What about the baby's father?"

"He's the one who divorced her."

Graham rubbed his hands together like a B-movie mad scientist. "It gets better and better."

"What are you blathering about?" Jason jerked the door open, sending Graham lurching back.

"She's a woman without a husband and father for her baby. You've already had practice filling those roles and just happen to be, uh, unemployed in that respect, if you will."

Jason glared at his friend. "I have a family already."

"Well, yes. But with Kinsey in Paris right now…" He held out his hands, as if Kinsey's absence explained everything.

"I'm suing for custody of Kinsey. I'm hoping she'll be back with me by the summer."

Graham raised his eyebrows but said nothing, though he continued to study Jason.

"What?" Jason finally asked when they reached his office.

"I'm waiting to hear more about Ms. Shelton—Diana."

"She came highly recommended as a designer of playscapes. She's agreed to work up some designs for us."

"Are you thinking of asking her out?"

"No. Why? Do you think I should?" He *had* enjoyed his time with Diana—more than he'd enjoyed anything in a while. But did he really want to get involved with anyone right now—especially a woman who might not really be his type?

"I think you should," Graham said. "If not her, someone. I think you need to start dating again. To find a good woman and fall in love and get married again."

"Get married again?" Even the word *married* felt awkward on Jason's tongue. He sank into the chair behind his desk. "Why would I want to do that? I've only been divorced a year."

"I'm not saying you should rush to the altar," Graham said. "But look at you. You're a family man. You're not going to be happy playing the swinging bachelor."

The truth of Graham's words stung. Jason loved being a father more than anything he'd ever done. He needed Kinsey back in his life every bit as much as his daughter needed him. But he wasn't so sure a new wife belonged in the picture.

"We both know dating can be slow torture," Graham

said. "The best thing for you is to find a good woman, marry her and start having babies."

"Babies! Graham, are you nuts?"

"A new family will help ease the pain of being separated from Kinsey."

"I told you, I'm going to fight for custody of Kinsey."

"And if you lose?"

"This isn't like getting a new puppy to replace one that ran away," he protested.

"No. It's about filling your life with the things that make you happy."

Jason shook his head. He refused to think of failure. But even if Kinsey didn't come to live with him full-time, he still had to think of her well-being. "I'm not sure I'd want Kinsey to have to deal with a new step-mother on top of everything else." Hadn't Diana pointed out how hard it had been for her stepdaughter to deal with Diana's presence in her life?

"Children are more adaptable than you give them credit for," Graham said. "Kinsey might even like having a stepmother. It's not all like in fairy tales, you know."

"I won't risk hurting Kinsey." Not any more than she'd already been wounded by the divorce and their separation. He liked Diana—a lot—but now wasn't the right time to rush into anything. Right now, he'd put all his energy into finding a way for him and his daughter to be together again.

STEVE AND HIS PARTNER, Eric, lived in a loft in the center of lower downtown Denver—LoDo, as it was popularly known. Visiting them always made Diana feel she was stepping into the kind of fantasy world frequently featured in upscale lifestyle magazines, a world of exotic wood, polished steel and impeccable cleanliness. Everything here was stress-free and perfect, or at least that was the way the two young men made her feel.

"Diana, you look wonderful." Steve greeted her with a hug and led her to a plush sofa. Of the two brothers, he looked the least like his father, having his mother's slender build, boyish features and dark blond hair, while Marcus and Richard were classically tall, dark and handsome. "How are you feeling? Here, why don't you put your feet up?" Before she could answer, he was lifting her feet onto an ottoman.

"This is a nonalcoholic cocktail." Eric put a pink, fizzy drink into her hand. "Full of antioxidants and vitamins."

"I feel fine," she said, accepting the drink and Eric's kiss. "But I won't complain about you two spoiling me."

"You deserve to be spoiled." Eric sat beside her. "How's our little girl?" He nodded to her belly.

"Very lively today. She's been kicking up a storm."

"She's ready to get out into the world," Steve said. "Are you ready for her?"

"Not really." She sighed. "I still need to get a car seat and take the hospital's childbirth classes. And pack my bag and choose a pediatrician and probably a lot of other stuff I'm forgetting." She'd always been a bit disorganized and a procrastinator. Impending motherhood hadn't changed that. Her carelessness, as he'd called it, had driven Richard crazy. One more reason she wasn't eager to change.

"And you need to register for gifts." Eric offered her a tray of canapés—diamond-shaped puff pastry topped with a dollop of whipped cream cheese and a sliver of roasted red pepper.

"Register?"

"For the baby shower, silly," Eric said. "People will want to know what to bring."

"Baby shower?" She looked at Steve.

"The shower we're giving you in two weeks," Steve said, grinning. "We wanted to surprise you."

Tears pricked her eyes. Damned pregnancy hormones. She cried at the drop of a hat these days. "That's so sweet, but you don't have to do that."

"We *want* to," he said. "Margery's helping." Margery Wright was Diana's best friend, as close as any sister could have been.

"Margery's putting together the guest list, but if there's anyone you want us to include, just let us know," Eric said. "And register for gifts somewhere. There must be a lot of stuff you need."

"I have some things—a baby bed and dresser with changing table." Also the music box and a few outfits she hadn't been able to resist purchasing.

"What about a stroller?" Steve asked. "Or a swing? You mentioned the car seat. A baby monitor?"

"Are you going to use cloth or disposable diapers?" Eric asked. "A diaper bag, baby bathtub, toys?"

She laughed. "How do you two know so much about it?" she asked.

"We've been researching," Eric said. He looked at Steve.

"We're hoping you'll let us babysit sometime," Steve said. "It'll be good practice."

"Practice?"

"We're talking about adopting. Nothing certain yet," he hastened to add. "But we're looking at the possibilities."

"I think that's wonderful." She hugged him, and reached out to clasp Eric's hand. Then she sat back and shook her head. "Claire will have a fit."

"Claire's always having fits," Steve said. "Has she been giving you a hard time?"

"Nothing I can't handle. She's just being Claire." Even as a little girl, Claire hadn't been shy about letting Diana know exactly what she thought of her, and most of it wasn't good.

"She's always been jealous of you," Steve said. "She never said anything about wanting a baby until you became pregnant. Now it's all she talks about. It's probably driving Derek crazy."

"Derek is a good guy," Diana said. "He really does love Claire."

"He'd have to, to put up with her craziness," Steve agreed.

"I was having lunch in Evergreen yesterday and ran into her," Diana said. "She wants me to look after Baxter while she and Derek are in Saint Lucia."

"Her babymoon." Steve rolled his eyes.

"What exactly *is* a babymoon?" Diana asked.

"I thought it was supposed to be a last romantic trip before kids come along," Steve said. "But Claire says it's a getaway focused on conception. This resort has special meals and exercises and things designed to foster fertility. Leave it to Claire to make something as enjoyable as sex into a competition."

"She and Derek have been married five years," Diana said. "Maybe they've been trying to have a baby for a while and she's starting to feel a little desperate."

"She's only twenty-six," Steve said. "She has plenty of time."

"Not every woman wants to wait until she's forty to have her first baby," Diana said.

"Not every woman has a husband who doesn't want children," Steve said. "Even the ones he already has."

"Oh, Steven." She squeezed his hand.

He shook his head. "I'm over it." He looked at Eric. "We're better off without him in our lives."

She bit her lip, holding back empty words of comfort that were second nature by now. She'd spent eighteen years trying to make up to the children for Richard's slights. But they'd seen through his behavior long ago. If Steve had ever wondered about his father's true feelings, Richard had made them clear when Steve had come out. Richard's first response had been anger. Now he chose to ignore reality altogether. He referred to Eric as Steve's roommate and had been known to hand out Steve's phone number to young women and urge them to contact his eligible son.

"I'm still furious at him for the way he treated you," Steve said. "Not to mention the baby you're carrying."

"Don't," Diana said. There was no sense going over this again. "It's better this way. For everyone."

"It is." Eric stood. "Dinner's ready. Why don't we eat?"

Over a four-star meal of chicken piccata, fresh asparagus and rice pilaf, they talked about Eric's latest commission to design a group of row houses in the Stapleton development, and Steve's work as a researcher at the National Renewable Energy Laboratory in Golden.

"What were you doing in Evergreen?" Eric asked as he served dessert—crème brûlée with a golden crust of caramelized sugar.

"I have a new client there—or at least I hope it's a new client. I'm drawing up some plans for a playscape for the Evergreen Montessori School. The superintendent and I were having lunch."

"Claire already called to report she'd seen you having a 'cozy' lunch with a good-looking man," Eric said.

"Cozy?" Was this another example of Claire overdramatizing, or had Diana allowed her attraction to Jason to be a little too obvious?

Steve laughed. "You look like you just got caught with your hand in the cookie jar. So, what's the story with this guy? Was the lunch cozy?"

"It was a business lunch." She fought down the blush that threatened to warm her cheeks. "Honestly, don't you

think the last thing I want—or need—right now is a relationship? I mean, I have a business to run and a baby
to get ready for. Besides, I'm enjoying being single
again."

"You're right," Steve said. "Relationships are so
much trouble. All that support from another person, di-
viding the workload, having someone waiting for you
to come home—"

"All right, all right. I get it." She smiled at him. "But
you can understand why I'm not eager to rush into anything, can't you? Maybe once the baby is here and I feel
more settled, I'll consider dating again. But I like the
idea of relying on my own resources for a while first."
At one time, the idea of letting someone else take care
of her had seemed like pure paradise. After years of having no one to rely on but herself, Richard's maturity and
reliability had been as much of an attraction as his looks.
In those days, she hadn't seen surrendering her independence as so much a sacrifice as a reward.

A reward that had decidedly tarnished over the years.

"I think you're being smart," Eric said.

"You are," Steve said. "And you're doing a great job
on your own. And you have friends like Margery and
us to help you whenever you need it."

She blinked back tears again. Maybe her marriage to
Richard hadn't been the best thing ever to happen to her,
but she could never call it a total waste. Not when it had
given her this baby, and Steve and Eric and Steve's
brother, Marcus. Even Claire, in her irritating way, had
shaped Diana's life, helping her to develop a thicker

skin and deal with criticism. "Everything works for good" was a cliché, but in her case she had to believe it was true.

# CHAPTER FOUR

JASON TOOK EXTRA CARE with his appearance the day of his scheduled meeting with Diana. He wore a tie Candace had always said made his eyes look bluer, and debated skipping out of work for an hour in order to get a haircut. He felt a little foolish, even as he knotted the tie and decided against the haircut. Why did Diana, of all people, excite this kind of interest? Was he some kind of deviant, turned on by pregnant women?

At ten minutes after one, Evie ushered Diana into Jason's office. "I'm sorry I'm late," Diana said as she took the chair he offered, and dropped her purse and portfolio on the floor beside her. "I didn't allow enough time for traffic coming up from Denver."

People who weren't punctual—Candace had never arrived anywhere on time in her life—usually annoyed him. But Diana looked so beautifully flustered, her cheeks flushed and hair curling around her face, that he couldn't feel anything but pleasure in seeing her again. "That's all right," he said. "Can I get you anything? Water or some tea?"

"No, I'm fine." She picked up the portfolio and unfastened the snap at the top. "Is there a table where we can spread this out? I have some drawings to show you."

"There's a workroom down the hall that has a large table."

In the workroom, she opened the portfolio to reveal a pen-and-ink and watercolor drawing. A notation at the bottom identified it as "Proposal for Evergreen Montessori School." If not for this, Jason might not have recognized his own campus.

He studied the illustration, which bore little resemblance to the playground currently in use at the school. Instead of the metal jungle gym there were several treelike structures, complete with green canopies that resembled clusters of leaves. Walkways and tree forts connected these structures, which were reached via ladders or climbing walls. Slides curved at either end, terminating in sandpits. Swings hung from the tree's branches. Nearby sat a tepee, a log cabin playhouse and giant wooden cutouts that mimicked the peaks of the mountains that surrounded the town. Everything was done in shades of bright blue, purple and green, with a splash of yellow here and there.

"It's certainly very colorful," he said.

"But not garish," she said. "I used colors that are already prominent in the local landscape, but more vivid, to stimulate children's brains. And, well, because bright colors are fun, and a playscape should be all about fun."

"Are these supposed to be trees?" He indicated the towers at the heart of the structure.

"They're supposed to *suggest* trees," she said. "Children might decide they're trees in a fantasy forest, or camouflaged rocket ships or magic beanstalks. The idea is to provide archetypal shapes, but allow the imagination to fill in the blanks."

"What's with the tepee and the log cabin?"

"Those are additions that relate to the area's history. Plus, children love miniature houses and other structures. But both are optional. The main focus is the central piece. I call it the fun forest."

He recognized that this was a good design. It offered lots of activities and was the kind of thing he knew the board would be excited about. But it was so *different* from what he was used to seeing. He had a difficult time picturing it at *his* school.

"You're frowning," Diana said. "What is it you don't like?"

"It seems very...modern," he said.

"Yes. Usually when people are replacing an old-style playground, they're looking for something updated. Something children can get excited about."

"Yes, we want to update," he conceded. "But I was picturing something...smaller. More subtle."

"I could certainly tighten the scope of the project. Tell me what you have in mind."

"New equipment, of course, but more...traditional." He struggled to find the right words to express his vision. "I was picturing wooden swings instead of metal, and maybe a bigger slide and a seesaw..." His voice trailed away as her expression shifted to one of frustration.

"If you want a traditional playground setup constructed of different materials, you don't need me," she said. "That's not the sort of thing I do. I thought you understood that."

"Yes, but I had no idea your design would be quite so...bizarre."

He could almost feel the temperature in the room dropping. Her eyes looked positively icy at the word *bizarre*. But her voice was even when she spoke. "I'm sure you've watched children's programs such as *Sesame Street* and *Dora the Explorer* and *Clifford the Big Red Dog*, right?"

He nodded. Dora was a particular favorite of Kinsey's.

"And you know the kind of books they love, from *Where the Wild Things Are* to *Harry Potter*."

"Of course I know these things. What connection do they have to a playscape?"

"None of those shows or books are subdued or subtle. They feature big ideas and bright colors and wildly imaginative concepts. *Bizarre* concepts."

He saw her point, but the idea of having large blue and purple treelike structures in place of the familiar swings and slides still chafed. "Instead of tearing out the old equipment completely, couldn't we incorporate it into the new design?" he asked.

Her lips tightened. "That's not a good idea. For one thing, older equipment often doesn't meet today's safety standards. And instead of a cohesive design, you end up with something that looks like it was cobbled together out of leftovers." Her tone of voice made it clear she wanted no part of any such cobbling.

"All right, but there's one thing missing from here that I think is really essential to any good playground," he said.

"What's that?"

"There's no jungle gym." He tapped his index finger on the approximate location of the current climbing structure. "No monkey bars or climbing frame or whatever you want to call it." He'd spent many happy hours on such structures in his childhood.

"Jungle gyms really aren't safe," she said. "They account for a large percentage of injuries on older-style playgrounds. But as you can see, this design has a climbing wall and several ladders."

"Maybe you could find a way to make them safer."

"The climbing wall and ladders *are* safer, and they work best with this design."

Their eyes met and he felt that same thrill of attraction, intensified by their already heightened emotions. Her gaze dared him to argue with her further, and he was tempted to do so, if only for the sake of seeing her so energized. "Is this the only design you have for us?" he asked, fingering the edge of the sketchbook.

"This plan works best for the space and number of children involved," she said. "It also fits into your budget. I do have other views, however."

She turned a page to show a side view of the structures. She'd even penciled in figures of children playing—a girl on a swing, another waving from the tree fort and two boys on the climbing wall. "Your drawings are very good," he said. "But I'm still not sure we're ready for such a big change."

"Perhaps if you show it to your board, or whoever has final approval…"

"That would be me. Or rather, I do have a board, and I'll certainly consult them, but in the past they've always relied on my judgment for anything involving the school."

"So, what you say goes?"

He stiffened. She made it sound as if he was some sort of dictator. "Of course not. That's just how it's worked out in the past. They trust my judgment. I welcome any input they have to offer."

"Then I look forward to hearing what *they* have to say about my design."

"We have a meeting tomorrow. I'll be happy to show them your ideas. Then I'll let you know."

"Please do." She snapped shut her portfolio, leaving the drawings on the table. "Thank you for your time. I can see myself out." Then she left, with as much dignity as a very pregnant woman could muster.

Jason stifled a groan of frustration and exasperation. The meeting hadn't gone at all as he'd planned. Had he really said anything so terrible? Or were all artists overly sensitive about their work? He was only being honest with her about his impressions, and she'd responded as if he were some kind of Neanderthal who'd taken a club to her proposal.

He studied the drawings again. Maybe the colors wouldn't seem so bright in real life. And children did like color. He could see how the unusual shapes and interesting angles of the playscape would inspire creativity. Unlike the current playground equipment, each piece of which had a specific purpose, the components of Diana's design could each serve different functions.

So why hadn't he said any of this to Diana while she was here?

He groaned and turned toward the door, thinking he might catch her in the parking lot and apologize for his behavior. He could admit that he was sometimes slow to accept new ideas. But he was not a tyrant. He wanted what was best for the school and its students, and if the board members agreed that hers was a good design, that was all that mattered.

But he stopped himself from running after her. No sense in making himself look any more foolish than he already did. Maybe it was just as well this disagreement had happened. It put some needed distance between them. From now on, they'd interact on a strictly professional level and forget any thought of romance.

A tap at the door interrupted these thoughts. "Jason?" Beverly Polis stepped into the room. "I hope I'm not interrupting anything. Evie told me you were in here."

"No. You're not interrupting." He assumed what he hoped was a less-distracted expression. "What can I do for you, Mrs. Polis?" he asked.

"Please, call me Beverly." Her smile was warm. She was the picture of the beautiful, sophisticated woman. Nothing flamboyant or erratic about her. "I hope you don't mind, but I know the designer was scheduled to deliver her drawings for the playground this afternoon, and I was dying to get a peek at them before the board meeting tomorrow." Her gaze was direct, hinting that she had other reasons for wanting to visit him than simply seeing the playscape sketches.

"You just missed Diana—Ms. Shelton."

"I thought that might have been her I saw leaving." She shook her head. "I remember when I was that far along with my two pregnancies. I felt so awkward and unattractive." Whether the comment was meant to call attention to her decided attractions now or to Diana's awkwardness, Jason didn't care to speculate.

"The drawings are over here," he said, indicating the papers spread out on the table.

"Oh, my," Beverly said, moving closer. "What a clever idea." She studied each drawing for several seconds. "Look at all the different activities. And I love the colors."

"You don't think they're too bright?" he asked.

She turned to him. "Do you?"

"I'm not sure. I like some of the more subdued greens, and even some of the blues. But purple? Yellow?"

She regarded the drawings once more. "I see what you mean. That *is* a little jarring. But it probably wouldn't be a big deal to change them. What do you think of the design itself?"

"It's very creative," he said. "With lots of possibilities for play. But I'll admit I do miss some of the more traditional equipment."

"Of course. We should ask the designer to incorporate some more traditional structures. That's an excellent idea."

Rather than being pleased with her willingness to so quickly align her opinions with his own, Jason found her inconstancy annoyed him. At least Diana's anger had been honest, whereas he couldn't help feeling Beverly's agreement was only designed to flatter him.

"I know the board will be happy to support your opinions," Beverly said.

"I want to present these drawings to the board and hear their opinions before I say anything," he said. "This is their school. I'm here to carry out their directives."

She laughed, as if he'd made a joke. "You were hired because we trust your judgment," she said. "You're good at your job, so we don't have to worry about overseeing your every move."

Again, he should have been flattered by her confidence in him. Instead, he was reminded of Diana's apparent disdain for the autonomy he'd assumed in his job. "I want the board to take an active part in this decision," he said. "It's too big a responsibility to place on one man. Now, I don't want to keep you…" He walked her toward the door.

"I was hoping we might have lunch," she said. "To talk about the playscape some more."

"I'm sorry, but I already have lunch plans."

"Maybe some other time, then." She gave him an appraising look. "I don't want to come across as too forward or blunt, but I'd really like the two of us to get to know each other better."

So he hadn't read the signals wrong. She *was* interested in him, but he felt…nothing. Not arousal or interest or anything but embarrassment that he wasn't responding at all to these overtures from this attractive, intelligent woman. What was wrong with him?

At least he had it together enough not to want to lead a woman on. "I really appreciate all you do for the school," he said. "I wish all our parents were as involved."

"I'm not speaking merely as a parent here," she said. "I really like you and I'd like to get to know you better—on a personal basis."

She wasn't going to make this easy, was she? "I'm flattered," he said. "And if I were in any other position, I might take you up on that offer. But I don't think it's a good idea for us to get involved. I'm in a position of authority over your children and susceptible to charges of favoritism."

"Surely no one would think that about you," she said. "And it's not as if you're a teacher or an aide who works directly with the children."

A valid point, but he didn't dare budge. Better for her to think he was a stickler for petty rules than completely uninterested in her. "I'm sorry." He offered an apologetic smile. "I really am flattered, but I can't risk it. You wouldn't believe the stories I hear when I get together with other school administrators."

She looked disappointed. "I suppose that's the results of the litigious society we live in." She squared her shoulders and he allowed himself a sigh of relief. He should have known Beverly would be reasonable about this. Her practical nature was one of the things he really liked about her.

She headed for the door, but paused halfway across the room and looked back over her shoulder. "Don't think I'm giving up so easily. After all, in two years both Max and Sophie will be in public middle school."

He watched her leave, torn between relief and regret. Two years was at once a safe distance away and surprisingly close. Who knew where he'd be or what shape his life would have taken by then? He liked to think he and Kinsey would be living as a family, happily ever after, as the storybooks said. But maybe those kind of endings only happened in fairy tales.

Yesterday's meeting with Scott hadn't gone well. The lawyer had explained that the fact that Candace was in France, married to a French citizen, complicated matters. Even if Jason won his case, if Candace refused to give up Kinsey, they could be facing a drawn-out and expensive legal battle.

Jason didn't want to put any of them through that, but dammit, Kinsey *needed* him. He had her best interests to think of, and nothing else mattered.

# CHAPTER FIVE

DIANA GRIPPED the steering wheel with white-knuckled hands and tried to concentrate on the traffic around her, but her head was filled with the image of Jason frowning at her drawings.

She'd worked so hard on those plans, hoping to impress him with her skill and creativity. She thought she'd outdone herself with the trees-and-mountains theme. She could imagine the excitement of the children and their parents when they saw the finished project.

But Jason had clearly not been excited. He'd regarded her plans as if she'd proposed bulldozing the forest surrounding the school and putting in a fast-food franchise, or filling the playground with old timbers and junk tires.

Then he'd made that announcement about the board going along with whatever he decided. A whole carillon of warning bells had gone off in her head when she heard that. She wouldn't have been surprised if he'd followed up by listing some of the many decisions the board had rubber-stamped. How many times had she sat through such recitations of Richard's many accomplishments?

She flipped on her blinker for her exit and eased the car down the ramp. Maybe it was just as well he didn't like her ideas. The last thing she wanted was to spend the next few months working with a man who was a younger version of the one she'd recently divorced. It wasn't as if she needed the work. She had plenty of other projects to keep her busy.

She didn't want to believe Jason was like Richard, but she'd be foolish to ignore the warning signs. She couldn't let physical attraction get in the way of common sense.

Which didn't make her disappointment at the sad end to her fantasies about her and Jason any easier to take. More than anything, she wanted to go home and curl up on the sofa with a chick flick, a box of tissues and a bowl of ice cream. But she'd promised Marjorie she'd meet her at the baby superstore to register for possible shower gifts. Diana had already put her friend off once; with the shower fast approaching, she didn't dare delay any longer.

"This is a nice surprise," Marjorie said, greeting her with a hug. "You're actually early. Excited about picking out things for the baby?"

"No, I'm tired and my feet hurt. I want to get this over with."

"Since when does shopping put you into such a foul mood?" Marjorie asked, following her into the store.

"I'm sorry. I've just come from an upsetting meeting with a client." A stubborn, arrogant, narrow-minded client.

Marjorie waited while Diana completed some paper-work and collected a computerized scanner gun that reminded her of the laser weapons featured in the science fiction dramas of her youth.

"Who was the client?" Marjorie asked as they started down the first aisle.

"Evergreen Montessori School. A man named Jason Benton."

"Ah. Your lunch date. I thought you rather liked him." At Diana's dark look, Marjorie offered an apologetic smile. "Steve told me. He seemed to think you and this guy really hit it off."

"We did. At least at first." She aimed the scanner at a pair of miniature pink tennis shoes, and it let out a series of beeps, as if she'd scored a direct hit. "I'm going to guess a man designed this thing," she said. "A young one, who's into computer games."

"What happened with Jason?" Marjorie asked.

"He hated my design for a playscape for his school."

"He hated it? He's a moron."

"Well, not hated." She honed in on a box of satin-covered clothes hangers. "He said it was *bizarre*." The word still hurt. He was lucky she hadn't been armed with a real laser gun. He might've ended up minus a few important parts.

"Then he's obviously not worth your time." Marjorie sighed. "Too bad. A good-looking single dad sounded like a good prospect."

"Why? Are you thinking of leaving Drew and finding a boyfriend?"

"Don't get smart with me," Marjorie said. "If you're going to meet an eligible man, the most likely way to do so is through your work."

"I'm not interested in finding a new husband." Margery and Steve's assumption that she *should* remarry was beginning to annoy her. Did they think she was incapable of looking after herself and her child alone?

She wasn't opposed to the idea of remarriage altogether, and she could admit she was lonely sometimes. But couldn't she take some time to enjoy being single first? "Now isn't a good time for a new relationship," she said.

"Is there ever really a good time?" Margery asked. "I'm not saying you should rush, but after so many years with Richard, you deserve a good man."

If Margery had meant the words to be comforting, they had the opposite effect. "Did everyone see how bad our marriage was but me?" Diana asked.

Margery compressed her lips into a thin line. "I'm not presumptuous enough to judge whether another person's marriage is bad or good," she said. "But I never thought you and Richard were an ideal match. You're warm and creative and fun and nurturing, while he always struck me as rigid and controlling and self-centered."

"He wasn't as bad when we first married," Diana said, feeling the need to defend her choice if not the man himself. "As he got older all his negative traits intensified. I used to be able to tease him into unbending a little, but lately he seems to view the whole world as if it revolves around him."

"I'm sorry you had to go through the divorce, but I think it could be a good thing for you."

Diana nodded. "I am happier now that I'm living on my own," she said. "I hadn't realized how...*confined* I felt. I'd spent so many years trying to please him and make him happy that I'd forgotten what it was like to do something solely because it was what *I* wanted."

Margery held up a frilly dress trimmed with yards of eyelet lace. "Right now, I think you should want this," she said. "I wish my girls were young enough I could still dress them. Now that they're teenagers, all I have to do is hint that I like something and they immediately hate it."

"There are some adorable clothes for babies these days." Diana said, grateful to shift the conversation to less emotional matters.

"Have you thought of a name yet?" Margery asked. "I'm tired of referring to her as *the baby*."

"I'd rather not say."

"Does that mean you don't know yet, or you simply aren't telling?"

"I know. I've had the name for my daughter picked out since I was twelve years old." Even then, she'd known she wanted to be a mother. She'd kept the name locked safely away all these years, like a treasure too valuable to look at. After resigning herself to the fact that she'd never be able to use the name, she wasn't ready to share it until after she'd held her daughter in her arms and whispered it in the baby's ear.

"Can't you even tell me the initial?"

"Why? Are you planning on having something

monogrammed?" Diana laughed. "I think we have enough clothes," she said. "Let's move on to something else."

They wandered down an aisle filled with sheets, bumper pads and coordinating curtains. "Are your parents excited about their new grandbaby?" Margery asked.

"My mother is appalled that I'm pregnant at my age. She says she's too young to be a grandmother."

"How old is she?"

"Fifty-seven going on twenty-seven." Diana examined a set of Winnie-the-Pooh sheets. "She was only seventeen when I was born, so I think she's intent on making up for her lost youth now. She and Dad are living in some hippie commune in the New Mexico desert."

"What about your father? What does he say?"

"'I hope you don't expect us to babysit.'" Diana laughed at Margery's shocked expression. "That's the way my parents are," she said. "They're not the touchy-feely type." They had been upset over the news of her divorce from Richard, though she suspected that was largely due to the loss of his income as part of the family. Her parents were chronically short of funds and over the years Richard had bailed them out of several financial crises.

"What about Richard's folks?" Margery asked. "What do they think?"

"They both died when Richard was in his forties." Diana remembered attending the funerals, scarcely a year apart. Richard had been stoic, though later he had broken down, recalling how much he had been in awe of his father, and how close he'd been to his mother.

"Well, *I'm* thrilled about this baby," Margery said. "I'm looking forward to being the doting godmother."

"You'll be the best godmother any little girl ever had, I'm sure." Diana squeezed her friend's arm.

"What next?" Margery glanced at the store directory in her hand. "Furniture, toys, accessories, transportation, books…"

"I'm feeling a little overwhelmed." Diana nodded toward the baby strollers lined up five-deep in front of them. Folding strollers, jogging strollers, strollers for multiple babies, strollers designed to double as shopping carts. "There are so many choices and I don't know if I'm qualified to make the right ones."

Margery patted her shoulder. "Any choice you make will be the right one. You've always had good instincts. Besides, I'm here to help. My three children may not be perfect, but I've managed to raise them to adolescence without any major mishaps. Besides, you're not a complete novice. You helped raise Richard's three children."

"They were already half-grown by the time I showed up." Diana grasped the handle of a sturdy-looking stroller and rolled it forward. She tried to imagine her little girl sitting in the seat, and swallowed hard, emotion threatening to overwhelm her. "I still can't believe Steve and Eric want to give me a baby shower. I was blown away when they told me."

"They're terrific young men, and I think you can take some of the credit for Steve, at least."

Diana moved on to a folding stroller and studied the instructions taped to the handle, though she didn't really see the words. Six weeks and counting until her due date, and there were still so many things she needed to take care of before the baby arrived.

"Something else is bothering you, I can tell." Margery rubbed Diana's back. "Are you worried about the birth itself? You know I'll be right there with you. Believe me, I'm fully prepared to boss the doctors and nurses into doing whatever it takes to make you comfortable."

Diana smiled at the image of Margery—all five feet three inches of her—barking orders at hospital personnel like a curly headed, cherub-faced drill sergeant. "I've avoided thinking about labor and delivery much," she said. "But in the past few days, it's really hit me— I'm going to be raising this baby *alone*. It's just so…so *daunting,* to think of having that much responsibility for someone's life."

"Hundreds of thousands of women and men do it every year," Margery said. "And most of their children turn out perfectly fine."

"I know. But it's not how I pictured things working out."

"Has Richard contacted you at all, to see how you're doing?"

"Not even a phone call." Though Richard had once told her he wanted no part of this baby, she had never believed the man she'd once loved could be so callous.

"I'm sorry," Margery said. "Maybe he'll feel differently once the baby is born. He *is* obligated to pay support, isn't he?"

"Yes. I think that's one reason I haven't heard from him. He was furious when I insisted he had a financial obligation to his child." In court, Richard had argued that since this baby had not been his idea and he wanted no part of it, he shouldn't be required to contribute to its upbringing. The judge had shown no sympathy for this reasoning. He'd told Richard if he'd been that determined not to father more children, he should have had a vasectomy. Richard had visibly paled at the idea. Though he hadn't actually brought his hand down to cover his crotch, Diana knew he was thinking about it.

"It doesn't matter what he does," Margery said. "You're going to be a great mother. And who says you'll be a single parent her whole life? You could meet a wonderful man and remarry. You might even have more children."

"I don't know about that. I may have all I can handle, running my business and raising this baby. I'm not sure I want to add a husband into the mix."

"Don't let one grumpy school superintendent put you off all men," Marjorie said. "There are still some nice ones out there."

But Diana didn't want someone who was merely nice. She wanted a man who could be her partner, not her boss. A man who respected her opinions even if his feelings about a situation were different. She wanted a man she could depend on to be there for her—the way Richard hadn't been.

Margery pulled a stroller out of the lineup. "This is a good one. It got good reviews in a consumer magazine I picked up in my dentist's office."

"Then I choose it." Diana fired the gun at the tag on the stroller. She turned and aimed the computer gun at a car seat and then a carrier, then switched it off. "Stick a fork in me, I'm done," she declared.

Margery laughed. "Let's get some lunch. We can drink a sparkling water toast to independence and making your own choices."

It still thrilled Diana to know she now *had* choices. One day she might decide to remarry. When the time came, she'd choose a man who could appreciate her creativity and warmth, her playfulness and spontaneity and ability to nurture. Her next marriage—if there was a next marriage—would be a more equal partnership, based on love instead of ego, on generosity instead of selfishness, on mature affection instead of youthful infatuation.

TEN MINUTES AFTER BEVERLY left, there was a tap on the door and Graham leaned into Jason's office. "You ready for lunch?" he asked.

"Sure." Maybe taking a break would clear his head and help him think straight.

"Was that Beverly Polis I saw leaving just now?" Graham asked as he and Jason headed for the staff lunchroom.

"Yes. She stopped by to take a look at the designs for the new playscape."

"Her ex was a plastic surgeon, you know. I heard he did some of his best work on her."

Jason shook his head. He'd heard the rumor, too, but it wasn't wise—or polite—to speculate out loud about such matters.

"I also heard she recently split up with the Brazilian photographer she'd been dating, and is looking for someone new, preferably a family man who can be a good role model for her children."

"How do you know any of this?" Jason took a tray and started down the cafeteria line.

"My wife serves on the fellowship committee at church with Beverly." Graham helped himself to a turkey sandwich and a side of coleslaw. "Apparently between filling cups of punch and cutting up finger sandwiches, they talk about this stuff."

"But why are you telling me?"

The two men paid for their food and carried their trays to a corner table. "Because I think *you're* the family man she's picked out," Graham said.

Jason shook his head. "I told her I had a policy of never dating anyone connected with the school— teachers, board members or the mothers of students."

"I didn't know that. Is there something like that in the policy and procedures manual?"

"Not that I know of. But maybe there should be."

"In other words, you made that up to put her off."

Jason bit into his sandwich and ignored the question.

But Graham refused to take the hint and drop the subject. "Why would you want to put her off? She's attractive and smart, with a pleasant personality. I'd think the two of you would be a great match. She's nothing like Candace."

Jason frowned at his friend. "Are you saying you thought Candace was wrong for me all along?"

"No. In a lot of ways, Candace was good for you. You were more relaxed with her, and her creativity was a good balance to your logic. But the differences between you grew larger over time. I don't think you'd have that problem with someone like Beverly. The two of you have similar temperaments."

"I'm not interested," Jason said. "And even if I was, now is not the time to get involved with anyone. I'm gearing up for the custody battle."

"What's the latest from your lawyer?"

"Her attorney responded and Candace is furious. She called me last night to tell me."

"Ouch." Graham winced. "What did she say?"

"A lot of things that can't be repeated in a school full of children." Even without the profanity, Candace's rage had been a palpable heat transmitted through the telephone wires. She'd accused him of being selfish and vindictive, of trying to turn Kinsey against her, and of putting his own needs before those of his daughter.

This last accusation had angered him deeply, and the two of them had ended up shouting, then hanging up on each other. Afterward, he'd paced the floor, trying to process what had happened. Had Candace always been so abrasive, or had he merely never noticed before? And if *he* was being selfish for wanting Kinsey with him, what did that make her?

"No mother is going to give up her child without a fight," Graham said. "You knew that going into this."

"I had some small hope that Candace would see it was better for Kinsey to be in the home she grew up in, near friends she's known all her life," Jason said.

"She's young," Graham said. "I'm sure she's already made lots of new friends in France."

"She told me she really misses her friends in Colorado."

Graham wisely changed the subject. "So what did the designer—Diana, was that her name?—what did she come up with for the new playground?"

"Playscape. It's a pretty wild design. These tall, tree-like structures that support swings, slides, a climbing wall, tree fort, ladder—all kinds of stuff. Very modern looking, with bright colors."

"You don't like it."

"I didn't say that."

"No, but I can tell by the expression on your face, especially when you said the words *modern* and *bright*."

"You make me sound like some grumpy old codger."

Graham laughed. "Maybe you are."

"After lunch, I'll show them to you. I'd be interested in seeing what another man thinks."

"What did Beverly have to say about them?"

"I think she liked them, but she was trying so hard to match her opinion to my own, it was hard to tell."

"All right, then what did Diana think of your reaction?"

"She was upset. I think she felt insulted."

"Then I definitely have to see the design that prompted such discord."

When they'd finished eating, Graham followed Jason back to the conference room. He reviewed the drawings of the proposed playscape, pausing some time before each, his expression serious, revealing nothing.

"Well?" Jason finally asked. "What do you think?"

"I think they're brilliant. The kids will love them." He turned to Jason. "When can we start work?"

"Diana has to agree to work for us first."

"Did you really upset her that much?"

"She wasn't too happy with me when she left here." He felt queasy, remembering.

"So you apologize," Graham said. "You were married long enough to get good at that, weren't you?"

Jason nodded. "You're right. If the board agrees with you and approves these plans, I'll call Diana and tell her I'm sorry, and beg her to work for us."

Graham shook his head. "This calls for more than a phone call," he said.

"What, then?"

"Ask her out. For coffee or lunch. Or if you're feeling lucky, dinner."

"Dinner sounds too much like a date. Stop playing matchmaker."

Graham looked a little *too* innocent. "I think you're capable of finding your own women. But the point here is that if you want Diana to work on this project, you're going to have to woo her. Show her you're serious about making this happen. And that means spending a little of that expense-account money on a nice meal and turning on the charm."

The idea of trying to charm Diana lifted Jason's spirits a little. Maybe over a quiet dinner he and Diana could get back to the friendly rapport that had characterized their previous interactions. "All right. I'll do it. After the board meeting."

"The board is going to love this." Graham nodded to the drawings. "They're exactly what we needed. A fresh perspective."

Right. And maybe Jason needed a fresh perspective, or at least a fresh start, with Diana.

# CHAPTER SIX

"IT WOULD HELP if they printed these directions in a language the average nonmechanical person could understand," Diana said as she struggled to fit the pieces of a mobile together. The mobile, designed to hang over the baby's crib, consisted of what looked like three dozen pieces of wood in primary colors, shaped like various animals. She picked out a blue one. "I think this is supposed to be a dog. Did you ever see a dog this color?"

She held up the object and her audience, a gray-and-brown miniature schnauzer, sniffed it cautiously. "It could be worse," Diana said as she tossed the piece back into the box. "The cat is pink."

The dog, Baxter, curled his upper lip in what was either a smile or a sneer. Diana looked at the jumbled parts in the box and sighed. "Why don't we take a break and have a snack?" she suggested.

Recognizing the word *snack,* Baxter jumped up and barked. Diana heaved herself to her feet and made a mental note to avoid sitting on the floor again. It would be really embarrassing if she had to crawl to the phone and call for a crane to get her onto her feet.

In the kitchen, Baxter had a jerky treat while Diana

washed down a handful of crackers with a glass of milk. Clair had delivered the little dog into her care the previous afternoon, on her way to the airport. "Don't forget to give him his thyroid pill with his meals, and he likes the canned food mixed really well with the dry, or he'll pick out all the canned stuff and make a mess," Claire said as she handed over food, toys, bedding and finally, the little dog himself.

"I remember." Claire rubbed Baxter behind the ears. "We're going to have a good time, aren't we?"

"I don't suppose you'll be in much shape to walk him, so if you want to hire someone to do it for you, I'll pay," Claire continued.

"I think I'm still capable of walking the dog around the block," Diana said.

Claire stepped back and eyed her critically. Diana had to force herself not to reach up and smooth her hair. "You are getting really big," Claire said. "Are you sure you aren't having twins?"

Diana didn't comment.

"Have you heard from Daddy?" Claire asked.

"No, should I have?"

Claire avoided meeting Diana's gaze. "He said he was going to call you."

"About what?"

"Oh, I'll let him tell you. I'd better go." She bent and kissed Baxter's nose. "Be a good boy. Mommy will see you soon." Then she was off, leaving behind a cloud of Chloe perfume.

Diana finished the last of the milk and watched Baxter drink from his dish. No word from Richard yet. Why would he call her after all this time? And why had he mentioned it to Claire? Unless, of course, it had been Claire's idea for her father to call. Maybe she was trying to get him to take an interest in his soon-to-be-born child. Maybe Claire, as her father's long-suffering daughter, sympathized with her half sister and hoped things would be better for her.

Right. As much as Diana wanted to think there were redeeming qualities in her stepdaughter, she doubted Claire would do anything to encourage more competition for her father's too easily distracted attention.

Diane could, of course, telephone Richard, but she'd refrained from doing so since the one time she'd called to ask him for the number of the auto mechanic they normally used. He'd refused to give her the number, then proceeded to repeat every complaint about her he'd already aired in court. She'd hung up and vowed never to speak to him again, unless absolutely necessary.

When the phone rang, it startled her so much she let out a shriek. Baxter jumped and began barking and dancing around her. She raced for the phone, attempting to quiet the dog as she did so. Half-afraid of hearing Richard on the other end of the line, she cautiously said, "Hello?"

"Diana? It's Jason Benton. I hope I'm not disturbing you."

"Jason." Relief that her caller wasn't Richard—and chagrin at the memory of her last less-than-pleasant meeting with the school superintendent—made her feel shaky. She carefully lowered herself into a kitchen chair and assumed a brisk, businesslike tone. "Have you made a decision about the playscape?"

"Yes. The board loved it and we want to hire you."

"They did?" She tried to keep the smugness from her voice, but it took some effort.

"Yes. And I made sure they all had the opportunity to express their opinion before I shared mine. Despite what you may think, I'm not a dictator."

"I never said you were." Though she *had* thought it.

"There are one or two small changes we'd like, and some questions some of the board members wanted to pass along. I was wondering if we might meet sometime soon to discuss them?"

"Certainly. I can come to your office later this week."

"I was hoping we could meet somewhere less formal. For dinner."

"I don't know about dinner." That sounded too much like a date.

"I feel I owe you, after the bad impression I made when you presented the drawings."

This suggestion of an apology softened her resistance. "You said my designs were bizarre," she said.

"A word I regret using. I was wrong. The design wasn't what I was expecting, but it wasn't bizarre. In fact, the idea is beginning to grow on me."

She almost laughed at his obvious chagrin. "That's good to hear."

"So what about dinner?"

"I don't know…." Keeping things strictly business between them felt…safer. More sensible.

But hadn't she spent the last eighteen years reining in her less-sensible impulses to please Richard?

Jason must have mistaken her silence for further resistance. "Humor me, please," he said. "I have an expense account and I seldom have the opportunity to use it. Plus, I'm growing really tired of my own cooking. You choose the restaurant. Anywhere you like."

"All right. Can we make it fairly early, say, six o'clock? On Thursday?"

"That sounds great."

"I'll see you then." She hung up the phone and looked at Baxter, who regarded her, head tilted to one side, as if prepared to be sympathetic to anything she had to say. "That was a very interesting and somewhat aggravating man," Diana said. "He wants to take me to dinner."

"Ruff!" Baxter signaled his approval of dinner.

She laughed at the little dog's enthusiasm, then laughed more as an idea formed in her mind. She knew a way to keep her meeting with Jason focused on business, while still allowing them to enjoy a meal together.

"WHERE DID YOU DECIDE we should go for dinner?" Jason asked when Diana arrived at his office Thursday—only seven minutes late this time.

"It's a surprise." She smiled at him and he decided that one look made all the groveling he'd had to do to persuade her to go out with him worthwhile. Even if this *was* supposed to be a business meeting, there was no reason he couldn't still enjoy himself.

"I'll drive," she said when he took out his car keys.

"I don't mind," he said.

"I'll drive," she said more firmly.

"All right." Was this one more way of asserting that this was definitely not a date?

She led the way to a dark blue Subaru wagon. As Jason opened the driver's door for her, a small gray-and-brown dog reared up in the backseat and barked at him.

"Baxter, be quiet!" Diana offered an apologetic smile. "He's harmless, I promise."

Jason walked around the car and slid into the passenger seat. The dog, Baxter, planted his front paws on the center console and regarded him seriously, nose twitching. "I didn't know you had a dog," Jason said.

"He belongs to Claire."

"I remember now. You promised to watch the dog while she was on vacation in Antigua."

"Saint Lucia." Diana started the car and backed out of the parking space. "And I didn't promise so much as Claire assumed I'd do it." She smiled at the dog. "But I don't mind. Baxter's a good boy."

The dog's stub of a tail quivered and his look turned adoring.

"I've thought about getting a dog," Jason said. He patted Baxter and was rewarded with another tail wag.

"They're good company," Diana said. "The house doesn't seem so empty when I come home and Baxter's there."

"There is that," Jason said. How many nights had he worked late as a way of putting off returning to his empty house? "I know Kinsey would love a dog, but it doesn't seem fair to leave an animal alone all day while I'm at work."

"Maybe you could bring him to work with you. The kids would love it."

He made a face. "I'm not sure how the parents would feel."

"If the dog was well trained and stayed in your office, I don't see how they could object," she said. "You could walk him on your lunch hour."

"Is that why Baxter is with us tonight? Because he doesn't like to be left alone?" Or because she felt the need of a chaperone, even a four-legged one?

"He does fine alone, but I thought he'd enjoy the outing."

Which wasn't really a satisfactory answer, but Jason refrained from pressing her.

She headed for the freeway leading toward Denver. With each passing mile he grew more curious. Had she chosen some favorite place in her neighborhood, or gone for broke and decided on some tony place downtown?

Confusion mixed with curiosity when she pulled the car to the curb in a quiet, suburban neighborhood. He stared at the neat rows of new-looking houses and the soccer fields to his right. "Do you live here?" he asked. An intimate dinner in her home certainly didn't fit his idea of a strictly business meeting.

"Oh, no. I live on the other side of town. Come on." She opened the door and somewhat awkwardly climbed out, then walked around to the back, where she took out a leash and pointed to a portable cooler. "You can carry that," she said, as she snapped the leash onto Baxter's collar.

Jason hefted the cooler and followed Diana and the dog down a path between the soccer fields. They walked through a small grove of aspens and emerged at a group of picnic tables set beside a playground.

The centerpiece of the playground was an undulating green-pink-and-yellow dragon. Its tail formed a curving slide and swings were suspended from its wings. Ladders led up to the head, where children peered out of the eyes and mouth and stood on a platform between the ears. Beside the dragon was a miniature yellow-and-blue castle with turrets and a drawbridge. Rope ladders and a climbing wall allowed access to the towers on either side, while the middle was given over to a playhouse.

"One of your designs?" Jason guessed.

"Yes. I wanted you to see the real thing in action." She began unpacking the cooler, laying out place mats, plates, napkins and silverware.

"What is this?" he asked.

"Dinner."

Baxter hopped up onto the picnic bench beside her and watched with great interest as Diana set out containers of pasta salad, cold chicken, fruit and rolls.

"Did you make all this?" Jason asked.

She shook her head. "I know a very good deli." The last item she took from the cooler was a covered dog dish. She set this on the ground and removed the lid. "This is your dinner, Baxter," she said.

The dog hopped down and sniffed the contents. Diana poured water into a second dish and set it beside the first. "There's a jar of lemonade and some cups," she said to Jason. "Would you pour the drinks while I serve the food?"

While they ate, he alternately watched her and the playground. Children laughed and squealed as they slid down the dragon's tail or swung from the wings. Two small boys used sticks as swords and battled from the castle's turret, while two girls inside appeared to be having a tea party. Diana watched the children and smiled. Was she pleased that they enjoyed her design, or was she thinking of her own long-awaited child?

"You have to admit," she said after a while, "this design makes the colors I chose for the playscape at your school look almost subdued."

"Yes," he agreed. "And the dragon is much more out-there than a group of trees and a tepee." He watched a boy and girl chase each other around the castle, both squealing with glee. "I still miss a jungle gym," he said.

"Was that your favorite when you were a boy?" she asked.

"Yes." Strange, he hadn't thought of his early love of climbing in many years. Talk of the new playscape had triggered a lot of old memories. As a boy, he'd loved anything to do with climbing—from scaling the height of his school's jungle gym to scrambling up rocks near his family's mountain cabin.

He'd put all that behind him as a teen and hadn't thought of it much since—until Diana had shown up to stir all manner of tumultuous emotions.

"What about you?" he asked. "What was your favorite part of the playground?"

"Mine was the swings." Baxter jumped up beside her and she began absently stroking his ears. "I would push myself as high as I could go and imagine I was flying."

He had a sudden image of her, small and bright-eyed, with her soft brown hair streaming behind her as she soared toward the sky. He would have been the boy on the top of the jungle gym, balanced there watching her, impressed by her daring and wishing she would look over and notice him.

"Come on," she said. "Baxter needs a walk, and I need to use the restroom. They're just across the park."

They walked slowly across the velvety, manicured grass, Baxter on a telescoping leash that allowed him to wander from side to side, sniffing bushes and fire hydrants and lifting his leg to mark the same. At a stone-sided building that had been painted to match the playground castle, Jason held the dog's leash while Diana went inside to use the facilities.

She emerged with one hand pressed to the small of her back.

"Does your back hurt?" he asked, keeping hold of the leash as they walked toward the picnic tables.

"If it's not my spine, it's my feet. Or I have indigestion." She shook her head. "Pregnancy is definitely not for wimps."

Candace had suffered similar aches and pains. Those days seemed so long ago now. Almost as if they'd happened to someone else entirely. "Have you picked out a name for the baby?" he asked.

"I have. But it's a secret until she's born."

She was a woman with a lot of secrets. Unlike Beverly who, he sensed, would have told him anything she thought he wanted to hear, Diana held things back. While she'd been open about her husband's abandoning her when she became pregnant, she hadn't said much about how she felt about this. At times she sounded almost glad the marriage had ended, at others her feelings were less clear. Her reticence added to her mystery and fed his curiosity to know more.

They reached the picnic table and sat once again. "You said on the phone that the board had some questions for me?"

"Oh. Yes." He'd almost forgotten the purpose of the meeting. He pulled a notebook from his pocket and for the next half hour went over the areas the board had asked him to address.

She took notes and answered all his questions. "You also mentioned some changes you wanted in the plans?" she said.

"Yes. We'd like you to mute the colors a little, and take out the tepee."

"I can make a good guess where the plea for muted colors came from," she said.

"You can still use the blues and greens, but maybe

add some browns, and make everything not quite so bright."

"I'll see what I can do."

"I think that's everything," he said, closing his notebook. Twilight was falling fast and they were the only ones left in the park. "What now?"

"Dessert."

"And that would be?"

"Ice cream. I know a wonderful place not far from here."

He helped her gather the picnic things and carry them to the car. Baxter jumped in the back and Diana drove to a storefront that advertised gourmet ice cream. They each ordered cones and ate them sitting at a small table in the glow of the outdoor lights.

Jason was hit with the sudden memory of him and Kinsey, laughing and eating ice cream cones as they walked along the Seine.

"What's wrong?" Diana asked. "You suddenly look so sad."

He hesitated. Was he revealing too much, to share his secret sorrow with her? Then again, her understanding and sympathy might make this easier to bear. "I was thinking of Kinsey," he said. "The last time I had ice cream, I was with her."

"Have you talked to her lately?"

He nodded. "We have a regular Saturday telephone date."

"But that's not really enough, is it?"

"No." He squared his shoulders, determined not to

give in to the depression that always threatened whenever he let himself dwell on thoughts of his daughter too long. "I have a friend who's going to set up a webcam for me, and we'll send one to Kinsey. Of course, I'll have to depend on her mother or Victor to set it up. Considering how her mother feels about me right now, that might not happen."

"Oh?"

A single syllable, spoken with such empathy it invited confidence. "She and I had a fight on the phone after I talked to Kinsey. She's not happy about my attempt to gain custody."

"Did you really think she would be?"

"I was hoping…" He shook his head. "I don't know what I thought, except that maybe she'd see this was better for Kinsey. And maybe I thought with her new marriage and her career taking off, she wouldn't mind so much not having full-time care of a child." As Diana's frown deepened at his words, he hastened to add, "I know that makes her sound like a horrible mother, and she isn't. But I'd like to make this as easy on Kinsey as I can, and if her mother and I continue to have shouting matches on the phone, *she's* the one who will be hurt the most."

Diana opened her mouth as if to say something, then shook her head.

"What is it?" he asked, steeling himself for her censure. She'd made clear at lunch the other day that her sympathies did not lie entirely with him.

"Nothing," she said. "Richard and I had some conversations like that when we were divorcing. Not pleasant."

"And since then?"

"I haven't heard from him. Though Claire tells me he intends to call."

"Do you want to hear from him?" Did she still have feelings for her ex?

"He's the father of my child, so for her sake, I'd like him to be a part of her life." She mopped a drop of ice cream from the table with a napkin. "Then again, I know he hasn't been a good father to the children he already has, so maybe it would be better for her if she was out of his life altogether."

"You might remarry and that man would be a father to her."

"Maybe. But I'm not in a hurry to find someone. I like having my independence. Making my own decisions. I don't know if I'll be willing to give that up again." She tilted her head and regarded him thoughtfully. "What about you? Do you think you'll remarry?"

"Not until Kinsey is older. I don't think she should have to deal with a stepmother on top of everything else."

"Not all of us are wicked, you know."

"I didn't mean…" Then he saw she was smiling at him, and he realized she was teasing.

"If you didn't have your daughter to consider, would you want to remarry?" she asked.

He hadn't thought about the matter much; he'd been too busy getting through the divorce and dealing with his daughter's move. But the idea held a strong appeal. "Yes," he said. "I think so. I enjoyed being married."

"That's good to hear. I think I enjoyed it in the early days, when I was still naive and filled with romantic notions."

"You don't have romantic notions now?"

Her smile was rueful. "Not when it comes to marriage. I'm afraid my experience with Richard has made me cynical."

"I'm sorry to hear that. I think you'd make someone a good wife."

She wrinkled her nose. "That's part of the problem. I spent a lot of years trying to fill that role, and in the end decided I didn't want such a narrow definition for my life. I wanted more."

This sentiment was so like something Candace had said to him near the end of their marriage that he had an eerie sense of déjà vu. "No one should define themselves—or be defined—by just one role," he said carefully. "Not by their job title or as a parent, spouse, sibling or friend. Each is only one part of our lives."

"I think my problem was I put too much emphasis on the wife role as being essential to my happiness," she said. "It's made me cautious, I suppose."

On this note, they headed back to the school.

"Thank you for dinner," he said, as they sat bathed in the glow of the school parking lot's security lights. "It was delicious, and I enjoyed seeing the dragon playscape."

"I hope I managed to ease some of your fears about my plans for your school," she said.

"Some. But I feel I still owe you dinner."

"Don't be silly. You don't owe me anything."

"How else will I justify my expense account if I don't spend some of it wining and dining contractors?"

The shrill ring of her cell phone prevented her from answering. "I'm sorry," she murmured, groping in her handbag for the phone. She flipped it open and frowned at the screen.

"Go ahead and answer it," he said. "I don't mind."

"I don't think I will." She closed the phone and slid it into her purse.

"Is everything all right?" he asked. She looked upset.

She shook her head, then nodded. "Oh, I'm sure everything's fine." Her eyes met hers, dark with distress. "It was Richard. I can't imagine what he wants, but it can't be anything good."

It was after nine o'clock by the time Diana returned to her house. Too late, she reasoned, to return Richard's call. She had enough trouble sleeping lately without the stress of a fight with him preying on her mind. And any conversation with Richard was bound to end in a fight.

In their marriage they had seldom disagreed. At the time, she'd told herself disagreeing with him would be petty; what did she care, in the grand scheme of things, what movie they saw or where they went on vacation? Better to humor him and keep the peace for the sake of the children—even after the children had grown and moved away.

Now, every buried grievance she'd ever had against him surfaced at the sound of his voice. Every past slight or former hurt came back to her in vivid clarity. As his wife, she had kept her mouth shut. Now she gave free rein to every emotion, anger being the most prevalent where he was concerned.

"I don't want to get into it tonight," she told Baxter, settling onto the sofa with the day's mail.

The little dog jumped up beside her, his brown eyes full of understanding.

She set aside the bills and slit open a square, pink envelope, and withdrew a card that made her laugh out loud. A row of elephants danced across the front of it, each carrying a different-colored umbrella. "I thought you might like a copy of the invitation for your baby book" was scrawled in Steve's hand on a sticky note affixed to the card.

"He's assuming I actually *have* a baby book," she told Baxter. "I guess I should add that to my growing list of things to be done before the baby arrives." She still needed to sign up for the birthing classes at the hospital, though she supposed if she never got around to it, she'd somehow manage to have the baby anyway. Women had been giving birth for centuries without instruction, hadn't they?

At least she'd gotten things settled with the Evergreen Montessori School. The changes they wanted were minor enough that they didn't require drawing up new plans. The budget was set and a time frame agreed on. She'd have to deliver the final contract for Jason to sign, but she had a boilerplate document on her computer she only needed to modify slightly for him. Once it was signed, she'd contact her contractors and schedule the work. Construction should be well under way by the time the baby was born. All she'd have to do was make a few site visits to monitor progress.

Which meant she'd be seeing a lot less of Jason. The idea made her sad. She'd only spent a few hours with him all told. Why should it matter if she never saw him again?

Yet she'd enjoyed the time she'd spent with him. She liked him—more than she'd thought she'd like any man again. He was smart and good-looking, a devoted father. He wasn't afraid to talk about his feelings or to listen to hers.

This might be enough to make her think seriously about pursuing a relationship with him, if not for other things that made her wary. He was obviously used to getting his own way—his statement that his board automatically approved all his decisions proved that. Then there were the comments he'd made about his wife's resistance to his attempts to regulate her life.

Having been there herself, why would Diana want to get involved with someone like him? Were his good qualities—the ways he was different from her ex-husband—enough to make her want to give up her hard-won freedom?

The phone rang, startling her out of her musings. She stared at the instrument as if it were alive, but made no move to answer it.

The answering machine picked up. "Diana?" snapped Claire. "Why aren't you answering the phone? Surely you aren't out at this time of night."

Sighing, Diana leaned over and picked up the receiver. "Hello, Claire," she said.

"Oh. There you are. What took you so long?"

"I don't move as swiftly as I once did," she said.

"I called to see how Baxter's doing. Has he missed me?"

"Baxter is doing fine, though I'm sure he misses you." Diana looked at the dog, who was snoring away at one end of the couch. She wondered if he thought of Claire at all. "How is your vacation?" she asked.

"It's been perfectly horrible. It's insufferably hot and humid and the beach is crawling with people. Derek got a terrible sunburn the first day. I told him to put on more sunscreen, but did he listen to me? Of course not. The food at this place is all vegetables and tofu and healthy stuff that tastes like ditch weeds. I haven't had a decent dessert all week and I would kill right now for a cheeseburger."

"I'm sorry to hear it's not what you hoped for," Diana said. She waited for more. She suspected Claire had more on her mind than her dog or the bad food at the resort. All the complaints about petty things were more likely the warm-up before she got around to really unburdening herself.

"Worst of all, I started my period the night we got here." Claire's voice quavered. She made a gulping sound and went on. "I've had horrible cramps and felt like crap, and how am I supposed to get pregnant with *this* happening?"

"I'm so sorry," Diana said, and meant it. She recognized the vulnerable, hurting girl beneath Claire's hard, sarcastic exterior. Though Claire had made no mention of wanting children until Diana announced her own pregnancy, it wasn't unrealistic for her and Derek to want children now, five years into their marriage. For someone like Claire, who had excelled at everything she'd ever tried, her inability to quickly conceive must have been frustrating.

"That is bad luck," Diana said. "But things will be better when you're home again."

"Yes, we'll be back in a couple of days. I never want to see this horrible place again."

"Do you need me to do anything for you in the meantime?"

"Could you keep Baxter a few days longer? I'm going to be too busy to look after him when we first get home. I have a doctor's appointment, and the decorator is coming to talk about new drapes for the den."

So much for Claire missing the dog. "Yes, of course. I'll be happy to keep Baxter as long as you like." His presence made the house seem less empty, and he seemed happy here.

"Did Daddy call you?"

Diana tensed. "I haven't talked to him," she said.

"That's odd. He promised he would call you."

"What is he supposed to call me about?"

"It doesn't matter. Thanks for looking after Baxter for me. I'll talk to you later." Before Diana could question her further she hung up.

Diana pondered this odd conversation. Claire had

sounded almost *guilty* about something. Had she put Richard up to it? But what?

Baxter moved closer and whined. Diana stroked his head. "Looks like it's you and me for a while longer, Baxter," she said.

He wagged his tail and rested his head on her belly, the picture of contentment. "You're right," Diana said. "We don't really need anyone else. We're happy just the way we are."

# CHAPTER SEVEN

JASON LOOKED FORWARD to Saturday afternoons, and his regular phone date with Kinsey. When it was one o'clock in Colorado it was eight in Paris. Kinsey would have just finished her supper and bath, and would curl up in a big chair to chat with her father. Jason always pictured her in her favorite pink-ruffled nightgown, her still-damp hair curling softly around her cheeks, smelling of baby shampoo and bubble bath, the way she always did when he'd been the one in charge of bath and bedtime.

In that too-brief thirty minutes they talked, the distance between them shrank and he felt a part of her life again.

"How are you doing, sweet pea?" Every conversation started the same, though her answers varied.

In her first weeks in Paris, Kinsey had responded sadly, with "I miss you, Daddy," or "I'm okay, I guess."

Lately, though, the sadness had faded from her voice. Now she said, "I went to my new friend Lizette's for lunch today. She has a little dog, a bichon, named Oscar, and we played with him."

"I've been thinking of getting a dog," Jason said.

"You should!" Kinsey said. "Then you could play with him when I wasn't there."

He wanted to ask her if she'd like to come live with him all the time, but he didn't want to put her into the position of having to choose between him and her mother. Not to mention Candace and her lawyer would cry foul if he made any mention of his custody motion to the girl. "I'm glad you've made a friend," he said instead. "How is school? Are you liking it better?"

Her former glumness returned. "Yes. Some." Her voice brightened. "We took a field trip this week. We went to a dairy and saw the cows. They were so beautiful, with velvety noses and brown eyes. Everyone in class was really impressed when I told them about the buffalo we have in Evergreen."

Jason smiled. The county managed a large buffalo herd not far from town. He had taken Kinsey there last spring to see the baby buffalo, perfect miniatures of their massive parents, scampering across the meadow. "I should send you some photographs to show the class."

"That would be good."

"Speaking of pictures, a friend of mine is helping me install a camera on my computer. We'll send one to you, too. Your mother can help you install it, then you and I will be able to see each other when we talk."

"Really?"

"Really."

"Victor will have to install it. Mama doesn't know anything about computers. Victor already taught me how to look up things on the Internet."

"What kind of things?"

"Oh, school stuff. And I have an e-mail address now. I can send you e-mail."

"That would be nice," Jason said, his stomach in a knot. *He* should be the one helping her with her homework and showing her how to send e-mail. Not some man to whom she wasn't even related. Jason forced himself away from such thoughts, back to his daughter. "I saw a friend of yours yesterday," he said. "Do you remember Megan? She said to tell you hi."

"I remember her. Did I tell you Lizette has a brother, Jean-Luc? He's fourteen and *sooooo* hot. Lizette says he thinks he's a real chick maggot."

"A chick what? Kinsey—"

"He told me I was cute, for an American girl."

What was a fourteen-year-old doing looking at his six-year-old daughter, much less telling her she was cute? And since when had Kinsey even noticed boys, must less *hot* older ones? Or did the French learn the art of seduction young? "I think you're too young to be paying attention to fourteen-year-old boys," he said.

"*Da-ad!* I'm almost *seven.*"

Too young. But before he knew it, she'd be seventeen, then twenty-seven. And he'd have missed it all. "Kinsey," he began again.

"I have to go, Daddy. Love you. *Maman* wants to talk to you."

*Maman?*

Candace came on the line. Her flat Midwestern voice now had a decidedly French accent. "Hello, Jason," she said. "How are you?"

"I'm fine. I miss my daughter."

"Yes. But you're still an important part of her life. She's not going to forget you, I promise. And you can telephone anytime. Or e-mail. Did she tell you Victor set her up with an e-mail address? The two of you can contact each other anytime."

She sounded so calm and reasonable, so different from their last conversation. Had her lawyer advised her to placate him this way?

"Phone calls and e-mail aren't enough," he said. "I want to see her."

"Are you seeing anyone, Jason? I mean, a woman?" Her voice had a light, teasing quality. "I think it would be good for you to start dating again. You're still young, good-looking, successful. I'm sure you wouldn't have any trouble finding someone."

*I wouldn't need anyone if you hadn't walked out on me,* he thought. "I don't need you to manage my love life."

"Brooding like this isn't healthy," she said firmly. "You need to get on with your life. Our marriage is over and I've moved on. Kinsey is here in Paris with me because I'm her mother and this is where she belongs. That's a reality you have to accept."

"I won't accept it," he said. *I can't.*

"Don't do this, Jason. Don't make me fight for our daughter in court. You won't win, and Kinsey is the one who will suffer most. When will you learn that you can't always have your own way? You couldn't in our marriage and I won't let you have it now, either."

"Goodbye, Candace. Kiss Kinsey good-night for me." He hung up, though his hand continued to clutch the receiver. It was warm in his palm, as if charged with all the emotion that had traveled over the line.

Once upon a time, Candace had been able to coax him into a better mood with her teasing. The very first time they'd met, he'd been angry because he'd gotten paint on his new suit—her paint, from a mural she was creating for the school where he was teaching at the time. He'd turned on her, prepared to berate her for her carelessness in not labeling the wet paint, and with one smile she'd disarmed him. She'd been recreating a scene from Antoine de Saint-Exupéry's *Le Petit Prince*. "Do you think the rose is beautiful enough?" she'd asked Jason. "I mean, is it so beautiful you could fall in love with it?"

The idea of loving a rose had never even occurred to him, and he had no idea how to answer her question. "It looks like most roses," he said. "I mean, I wouldn't have any trouble identifying it as such."

"But does it look like a particularly special rose?" A dreamy expression filled her wide green eyes. "Then again, it isn't really the beauty of the rose, is it? As the fox tells the Little Prince, it's the time he spends with the rose that gives the rose its importance."

He and Candace had spent a lot of time together after that. She was unlike anyone he'd ever known—so carefree and daring. Throughout his teens, his home had been in constant turmoil. He'd learned the importance of staying in control, of acting in response to reason rather than emotion.

He'd been drawn to Candace the way some people are compelled to climb mountains or ski down perilous slopes. When he was with her he felt more energized and daring. He'd been certain they would always be happy together, that she would be the color in his black-and-white world.

Unfortunately, the things that had excited him while they were dating began to grate on his nerves once they were married and together all the time. Carefree translated to careless, daring to reckless. He'd hoped having a child would settle her, make her more responsible, less flighty. Instead, she'd declared she was tired of being conventional.

She gave away all her business suits and began wearing gauzy dresses, sometimes with outlandish hats. She played opera CDs at top volume and moved her easel into the living room, saying the light was better in there. Jason was constantly stepping over and around canvases and boxes of art supplies, rescuing Kinsey from piles of oily paint rags or cleaning paint from her fingers and face. Exasperated, he'd once told Claire, "Normal people don't live like this."

She'd looked at him for a long moment, her green eyes like winter seas. "What made you think I ever wanted to be normal?"

She'd dismissed normal as boring and dull, but Jason needed normal. And children did, too. Normal was comfortable and safe—all the things a childhood should be.

Jason would do anything to make sure his daughter

was happy, including putting his own personal life on hold until Kinsey was older. Later, he hoped to find a woman to love—someone steady and dependable and logical. Someone more like himself, with whom he could be happy. He no longer thought love needed to be exciting, as it had been in the early days with Candace. Now he wanted something deeper, dependable and well-rooted enough to last forever.

DIANA DIDN'T RETURN Richard's call, and to her relief, he didn't try to call again. She drew up the contract for Evergreen Montessori School, but rather than mail it, she decided to deliver it to Jason herself.

"I'm sorry, but he isn't here," his secretary told Diana when she arrived at the school the following Wednesday afternoon. "You can leave the papers for him if you like."

"I was hoping to give them to him personally." Diana tried to hide her disappointment. "There are a few things I'd like to go over." The thought of seeing him again had buoyed her spirits all day.

"Well…" Evie studied her for a moment, considering something. "If you like, you could take the papers to him at home," she said at last. "He took the day off to deal with a repairman. By now, he'd probably appreciate the company." She grabbed a sheet of paper and began to sketch a map. "It's not far. It's a very nice house—too big for one man to be knocking around in by himself."

"Oh?" Diana could think of a dozen questions she'd

like to ask Evie about her boss, but no way to make them seem like anything less than a woman trying to get the full scoop on a guy who interested her. The truth, maybe, but not the professional image she hoped to project. So she feigned coolness while Evie sketched a map to Jason's home.

Diana found the house without much trouble, a dramatic A-frame with a bank of windows across the front that must offer a spectacular view of the snow-capped mountains in the distance.

She made her way up a stone walk, past empty flower beds and forlorn shrubs. Jason's ex must have been the gardener in the family. Everything about the yard was neat, but it lacked interest.

She rang the bell and waited, studying the single empty planter that was the only ornament on the other-wise bare front deck. The door opened and Jason stared at her. "Diana! What are you doing here?"

"I brought the contracts for the playscape." She hefted the folder of papers. "Your secretary said you were home today and wouldn't mind if I dropped by."

"Of course not. Come in." He held the door wider and stepped back to allow her entrance. "Excuse the mess. Some pipes busted and the plumber's been in and out all morning."

The house was in only mild disarray—a rug rolled up here, a chair shoved back there. The man was pleas-antly rumpled—his hair uncombed, the sleeves of his blue chambray shirt pushed to his elbows, the shirttails untucked and hanging over faded jeans. His feet were bare and Diana found herself staring at them—at the well-shaped instep and the light dusting of dark hair across his toes. The sudden flutter of desire within her caught her by surprise. Seeing him like this seemed so much more intimate than any other time they'd spent together.

"Let's go into the dining room." He led the way down a short hall into a room at the back of the house. Light spilled from another bank of windows, across polished wood floors, onto a Shaker-style table and chairs made of rich mahogany. A matching buffet sat along one wall, its top crowded with photographs in silver frames.

"This is beautiful," she exclaimed, rubbing her hand across the table, the polished wood smooth and satiny against her fingertips.

"Thanks." He offered her a chair on one side of the table. "Can I get you something to drink?" he asked. "Water, or tea?"

She debated asking for tea as an excuse to stay longer, but considering the minute size of her bladder these days, decided against it. "No, thank you."

He sat at the end of the table nearest her, their knees almost touching. "How have you been?" he asked, his gaze searching her face, as if to judge for himself the truth of her answer.

"I've been well. Busy. Trying to get everything done before the baby arrives."

"Is there anything I can help you with? I'm pretty handy with tools if you need any baby furniture put together, and I'm good for any heavy lifting."

The offer touched her. "Thank you, but my stepson Steve has done all that for me."

"Do you have your car seat yet?"

"Yes. I finally bought one, so I'm ready to bring the baby home from the hospital."

"Are you sure it's installed properly?" Jason asked. "Those connections can be tricky. I'll be happy to check it out if you like."

Again that flutter of desire. Not because his offer to see to the car seat was so sexy, but because his obvious concern and desire to help was. "Thank you, but I'm sure it's okay." She opened the folder between them, anxious for something to look at besides his gorgeous blue eyes. "I brought two copies of the contract. I'll need someone representing the school to sign both and I'll sign both, then you can keep one copy."

He patted his empty shirt pocket. "I'll need a pen."

"I have one." She handed him a pen from her purse. "I'll give you a few minutes to read over it, but I believe it includes all the information we talked about."

While he reviewed the contract, she looked around the room some more, all the while hyperaware of his warmth and masculinity scant inches away. How many years had it been since she was alone in a house with a man to whom she was not related? Obviously, she'd forgotten how to behave in such a situation. Her mind insisted on conjuring up images of Jason's bare feet, which led to speculation about what the rest of him might look like bare. She felt breathless and a little light-headed from more than the growing baby pressing against her diaphragm. She'd heard that some women experienced increased sexual desire during pregnancy, but this was her first encounter with such sensations. If she'd known Jason better, he might have been in real danger of her dragging him off to his bedroom and having her way with him.

Not that she was in any condition to carry out her fantasies, but a woman could always dream.

*The room,* she reminded herself. *Look at the room, not the man.* She shifted her gaze to the buffet. The pictures lined up along its top were mostly of a smiling blond girl, either by herself or with Jason. One photograph showed a slightly younger Jason cradling a swaddled baby. His joyful smile and the adoring look in his eyes made Diana's throat tighten. No man would ever look at her daughter that way—at least not while she was an infant.

Diana forced her eyes away from the photograph, onto another. This one showed a laughing toddler on a swing, flanked by Jason and a striking red-haired woman, her hair a cloud of curls, her eyes a deep sea-green.

"You've probably figured out that's my ex-wife, Candace."

Jason's voice startled Diana. She flushed, realizing he must have noticed her staring at the photograph. "She's very beautiful," she said.

"Yes. Kinsey takes after her." He finished signing the second copy of the contract and returned the pen to her. "I only keep that picture there because it's such a good one of Kinsey at that age. The photo at the end on the right side is the most recent I have of her, taken right before the divorce."

Diana looked at the eight-by-ten of a little girl with pigtails and a gap-toothed grin. She stared out from the picture frame with the charm and innocence of a child who had never known sorrow. "She's a beautiful girl," Diana said.

"Yes, she is. And getting more beautiful every day."

"How is she doing?"

"She sounds…good when I talk to her on the phone. She seems to be liking school more and she's making friends." He frowned. "Getting interested in boys. At her age, she should be interested in dolls, not boys."

Diana almost laughed at his obvious dismay. "I imagine both hold a certain fascination."

"She's learning more French, too."

"It's good to hear she's adapting so well."

"Yes, I suppose." He wouldn't say so outright, but Diana imagined it would have made things easier for him if his daughter hadn't been quite so happy apart from him. She searched for some way to ease the conversation to a less painful subject, and scanned the room for some other item of interest.

Her gaze came to rest on an oil painting on the opposite side of the room, an impressionistic scene of a mountain meadow done in purples, pinks and soft greens and browns. "That's a lovely painting," she said.

"One of Candace's," he said. "An earlier work. Her paintings now are more modernistic, but I like this style better. I kept it because it was one of Kinsey's favorites and I thought it might upset her if she came back and it wasn't here."

Back to Kinsey. Of course, she was probably never far from his mind. Unable to think of any words to comfort him, Diana once more attempted to shift the conversation to a different topic. "I'm keeping Baxter a few extra days," she said. "It seems Claire has too much on her plate right now to deal with the dog."

Jason cocked one eyebrow. "And I suppose she thinks you have all the time in the world."

"I don't mind, really. He's an easy little dog." She completed her signature on both contracts, then slid one copy to him and returned the other to her folder. "I'll call the contractor tomorrow and we can get started right away. He'll work as quickly as the weather allows, but you'll be without a playground for some time."

"We already have a plan to use the soccer field and the gym for some organized games and other activities."

"Good thinking." She stood and he rose also.

"Now that you're here, would you like to see the rest of the house?" he asked.

"I'd like that very much." She seized this excuse not to have to leave right away.

"Let's start at the front and I'll give you the ten-cent tour."

"How long have you lived here?" she asked as they retraced their steps to the living room where she'd entered.

"Almost ten years. Candace picked the place for the light and views and the architectural lines."

"She had very good taste," Diana said, as she gazed

at the soaring beams overhead. South-facing windows presented a view of the distant mountains and nearer foothills awash in light and shadow. Half a dozen elk grazed in the yard across the street, oblivious to drivers slowing to take a look.

"Yes. Though later on she grew bored with the place. She wanted to move closer to town, which made no sense with my job being so nearby. Of course, I realize now it wasn't Denver that attracted her so much, just her need for change. Paris suits her now, though eventually she'll probably tire of that, too."

"Some people are more restless than others." Diana was feeling pretty restless herself, with him standing so close to her.

"This little room back here was originally going to be Candace's studio, but later we turned it into a play-room for Kinsey." He led her into a mostly bare room. Built-in bookshelves held a collection of children's classics. A wooden rocking horse sat in one corner, next to a battered toy chest, abandoned and forlorn.

"This would make a nice library," Diana said. "Or a home office." Surely either would be better than this sad reminder of what might have been.

"I guess it would at that." His voice was steady, re-vealing nothing. "The kitchen is through this door."

The kitchen was small but gleaming, with black-and-stainless appliances and gray granite countertops. "We had it remodeled two years ago," he said.

"It's wonderful. Do you like to cook?"

"I do."

"Perfect. I like to eat." She knew she was openly flirting with him, but she couldn't seem to stop herself.

"Then maybe I should make you dinner sometime." His eyes held a new light—and a decided heat she hadn't seen there before. She took a step back. He hesitated a fraction of a second, then took a step forward. "You have an interesting effect on me," he said softly.

"Oh?" She held her head up, refusing to give in to the trembling nervousness that had overtaken her. "What effect is that?"

"When I'm with you, I forget all about anything else. You make me forget myself."

"That's interesting. When I'm with you, I'm even more aware of myself than usual." Aware of the way her body responded to his, of the sensual, sexual woman underneath the maternity clothes and sensible shoes.

She was aware of him, too—of the subtle, woodsy scent of his aftershave and of the tiny white scar in the left corner of his upper lip. She noticed the way his right eyebrow quirked upward whenever he smiled, and the way the pale blue cotton of his shirt cuffs contrasted to the golden tan of his skin.

She was very aware of being attracted to him, of her breath quickening as he stood so close to her, of leaning toward him, lips parted.

Their eyes met, and she saw her own desire reflected back to her. He put a hand on her arm, though whether to steady himself or to pull her close, she couldn't say.

He inclined his head slightly, and she waited, not daring to move.

Then she forgot about breathing or seeing or anything but the feel of his lips on hers. His arms wrapped around her, tucking her into the shelter of his body.

Only now could Diane admit how much she'd wanted this to happen. They kissed with the fierceness of desire too-long denied, savoring the taste and feel of one another. Every part of her was alive with a new awareness of him, and she reveled in discovering everything this new closeness revealed. The softness of his lips against hers contrasted to the masculine roughness of the five-o'clock shadow along his jaw. She squeezed his shoulders, reveling in the hard line of muscle, and breathed deeply of his spice-and-leather scent.

The pain of the past few months, of Richard's rejection and her fears about giving birth and raising her child alone, vanished in the magic of that kiss. Then the baby kicked, as if trying to kick away the man who held her so tightly.

Jason stepped back suddenly, dazed and blinking. He stared at her. "I didn't mean for that to happen," he said. "Forgive me."

An apology was not what she had expected. "I wasn't exactly objecting," she said. She couldn't remember when she'd enjoyed a kiss so much.

"No, that was out of line. I really shouldn't have…" He looked away. "Why don't we go back into the living room?" he said, only a slight roughness in his voice hinting that anything out of the ordinary had happened between them.

He left the room. Diana stared after him, irritation and frustration subsiding as reality erased the romantic fog the kiss had temporarily settled over her. Relationships had never been casual for her. When she involved herself with another man—*if* she ever wanted that kind of involvement again—she needed to do so with her whole heart. How was that even possible when all her emotion and energy right now needed to go to her new baby?

She took a deep breath, marshaling her resolution, and followed Jason into the living room. If he could pretend that nothing had happened between them, then so could she.

Later, when she was alone, she might take the time to examine that kiss, to savor the beauty of the moment and ponder what might have been.

## CHAPTER EIGHT

JASON HAD FORGOTTEN himself for those few moments in her arms, forgotten restraint and sense in the onslaught of longing and desire that had led him to give in to the compulsion to kiss her.

The kiss had been wonderful—erotic and moving and magical. But there was little to be gained by pursuing the matter further. No matter how much she bewitched him whenever he was with her, apart from her he could think of half a dozen reasons a relationship between them would never work. She was too independent. Too stubborn. They were both rebounding from wrecked marriages. She'd soon be involved with the demands of new motherhood. The more he thought about it, the more he was sure he was wise to not allow emotion to overrule logic.

Maybe he was being overly cautious, but the disastrous end of his marriage had convinced him he never wanted to put himself—or his child—through that again.

He studied Diana as she gathered her paperwork and prepared to leave. Was she relieved he'd walked away, or disappointed? Did she think he'd been rejecting her? Or would she have been offended if he'd suggested they move from kissing in the kitchen to a more intimate relationship?

She looked up and her gaze met his for a fraction of a second before sliding away once more. In that moment, he saw a flash of darkness and heat. Disappointment? No, more like anger. "Diana," he began, ready to defend himself.

She shook her head. "I'd better go." She rushed past him, cutting off any remark he would have made.

The door slammed behind her with a finality that recalled Candace's leaving. He slumped into a chair. He hated this feeling of not being in control of his own emotions. Why did he let Diana affect him this way? What was it in his character that led him to make a fool of himself over creative, unpredictable women?

The ringing doorbell stopped his spiral toward self-pity. Half fearful and half hoping that Diana had returned, he went to answer it. "What are you doing here?" he asked Scott Reisler as he opened the door.

"It's good to see you, too, Jason." The attorney moved into the living room and deposited his briefcase on the sofa. "I was on my way home and thought I'd be a nice guy and drop off the paperwork you need to sign."

"Thanks." Jason shut the door. "Sorry I was so abrupt. I was expecting someone else."

"Someone prettier than me, from the sound of your voice."

"Just a business colleague. Give me the papers and I'll sign them."

"Not so fast." Scott held up his hand. "Now you've

made me curious. Who was that woman I saw tearing out of your drive as I was pulling up?"

To his chagrin, Jason felt his face heat, but he did his best not to betray his feelings in his voice. "That was the designer who's overseeing the new playscape for the school."

"Oh? She looked pretty. What little I saw as she raced by."

"She's almost nine months pregnant."

It was Scott's turn to look embarrassed. "Sorry. I didn't realize she was married. I thought she was a new girlfriend or something."

Jason didn't bother to correct Scott's mistaken impression about Diana's marital status. "I don't think now's the time to start a new relationship," he said. "We want the court to see me as the devoted father who has no time for anything but his daughter."

Scott nodded and opened the briefcase. "Yes, there is that." He handed Jason a sheaf of papers. "This is the paperwork for the preliminary hearing on your custody motion. Your ex-wife will need to have an attorney licensed to practice in the United States and Colorado."

"She has an attorney." An expensive, ruthless partner in one of the top firms in the state, who specialized in divorce and custody cases. Candace had met him at an exhibition of her paintings at a trendy downtown gallery a year before the divorce. Maybe even then she'd been planning to leave. Once upon a time, Jason had thought he knew the way his wife's mind worked; now he realized how naive he'd been.

"Don't look so glum," Scott said. "I have some good news for you."

"Oh? What's that?"

"I have a friend, another attorney, who's worked with a private investigator in Paris. I had the P.I. run a background check on Candace's new husband and he came up with some useful information."

Cold fear gripped Jason. Was Victor a child molester? A convicted felon? "What is it?"

"Victor has two children of his own that he's had little or no contact with. One was the result of an affair with an actress seven years ago. She gave birth to a daughter after she and Victor broke up. He's only seen the girl a couple of times and pays no support. The other child is a boy belonging to his former landlady, a woman ten years older than him. He's still in touch with the boy, but again, pays no support."

"In other words, he's a deadbeat dad."

"The French don't use that term, but he certainly doesn't come across as good father material. That will definitely work in your favor."

Jason nodded. Scott probably meant the news to cheer him, but he didn't know what to feel. On one hand, neglecting to make support payments and being indifferent were a long way from molestation or other abuse. And while he didn't want Kinsey to be hurt by her stepfather's indifference, he could admit he was relieved Victor wouldn't be competing with him for Dad-of-the-Year honors.

"Don't knock me over with your gratitude," Scott said. "This is good news."

"Sorry, Scott. I appreciate everything you're doing for me, it's just—" He shook his head. "I never in a million years expected to be in this situation. I mean, I never pictured myself as the kind of man who would have to stoop to hiring a private detective in order to be with my own daughter."

Scott clapped him on the shoulder. "This wasn't something you could have foreseen," he said. "Nobody gets married and has kids with the plan to divorce. You can't predict how other people will behave."

Was that true? Looking back, Jason could see all the ways he and Candace had been wrong for each other. As early as their second date, when she'd showed up fifteen minutes late and suggested they blow off the symphony tickets he'd purchased and have a picnic at the zoo instead, he should have seen how incompatible they were. If he'd been more careful then, he could have avoided all this heartache now.

"I've learned my lesson," he said, as he began signing the legal papers. "My next relationship, I'm going in with my eyes wide-open. I'll find a woman whose personality is a better match for mine. I won't make the mistake of getting involved with someone so different again."

"Good luck with that resolution," Scott said. "Last I heard, love is blind. And the blindness can hang around awhile. My wife and I had been married three years before I knew how much she loved ballet. I mean, the woman is a hockey fan! Who knew she'd expect me to take her to Avalanche games *and* performances of the Colorado Ballet?"

Jason signed the last page and returned the stack of documents to Scott. "I'm not talking about likes and dislikes so much as the way two people see the world. I've always been very organized, methodical and logical, while Candace planned every day around her emotions. If she felt like going for a drive instead of cleaning house, she did. I remember coming home from work one day to discover she'd painted our master bathroom orange. When I asked her why, she said it felt like the right thing to do." One fear he had about Kinsey living with Candace was that she'd grow up as flighty and emotional as her mother. Candace's approach to the world worked fine for an artist, but almost any other career would demand more discipline and conformity. How was Kinsey to learn about logic and the rewards of hard work and all the other things she needed to know to be successful and happy if Jason wasn't the one to teach her?

THE BABY SHOWER at Steve and Eric's loft that Saturday was no mere cake-and-punch affair. The two men had prepared a mouthwatering array of gourmet munchies, and decorated with fresh flowers and satin streamers. "You sit here," Steve said, leading Diana to an upholstered chair with a footstool. "Tell me what you want to eat and drink and I'll bring it to you."

"I'm perfectly capable of getting my own food," she protested.

"But you're our guest," Eric said. "It's our turn to wait on you."

"Take advantage of it." Margery spoke around a mouthful of hors d'oeuvres. "You need more practice letting other people take care of you."

Feeling only a little guilty, Diana settled back into the chair and put her feet up. Coworkers, neighbors and even some of Richard's female university colleagues turned out for the event. Diana teared up more than once as she unwrapped the gifts Margery handed to her—tiny pink and white onesies, hand-knit receiving blankets, a soft infant bathtub and several months' supply of diapers. Steve and Eric presented her with a deluxe stroller that started a fresh flood of tears.

"If you don't like it, we can take it back," Steve said anxiously.

"I love it." She dabbed at her eyes with a handkerchief. "Don't mind me, it's just the hormones."

When the last gift was unwrapped and the giver enthusiastically thanked, Steve delivered a plate of cheese balls, puff-pastry-wrapped chicken, barbecue shrimp and other delicacies. "I can't thank you and Eric enough for this party," Diana said. "It's been wonderful."

"We had a blast putting it together." He propped himself on the arm of her chair. "How are things going? Do you have everything ready for the baby?"

"I think so. Margery and I only have one more child-birth class."

Margery settled into a folding chair beside Diana. "I'd forgotten how scary those classes could be," she said. "They tell you everything that can go wrong. If women had to take those classes before they got pregnant, no one would ever have a baby."

"I'm sure everything will be all right," Diana said, hoping she sounded more confident than she felt. The prospect of giving birth *was* frightening, both the labor and delivery itself, as was the prospect of caring for a helpless infant who would be totally dependant on her.

"Do you have everything arranged at work so you can take some time off?" Margery asked.

"I only have two projects right now—a park in Fort Collins that's almost done, and the playscape at the Evergreen Montessori School."

"I thought that project fell through," Marjorie said. "That the superintendent thought your design was bizarre."

"He changed his mind. Or his board changed it for him. The contractors should start work there next week." She hadn't seen Jason since that awkward afternoon when he'd signed the contract and they'd shared that kiss. That incredible kiss she thought about too often, especially during long, dark evenings. As much as she believed not letting things go further was the prudent thing to do, her mind insisted on playing endless games of what-if.

Since that day, she'd communicated with him through her contractor, telling herself she was being wise to avoid temptation. But the only messages she'd had from him came via his secretary, and she couldn't help being disappointed.

"Have you picked out a name for the baby?" Steve asked.

"Maybe she'll tell you." Margery scooped dip onto a chip. "She wouldn't tell me."

"I'm not telling anyone," Diana said. "Maybe I'm superstitious, but I want her to be the first one to hear her name." She nudged Steve. "Enough about me. Tell me what's up with your adoption application?"

Steve's smile broadened. "Our home study will be complete next week. Then it's a matter of waiting for a baby. Or a toddler. Though I know we'll both be nervous wrecks while we wait."

"I'm very happy for you," Diana said. She could identify with that excitement. She had never understood how Richard could be so callous as to not feel it, too.

The doorbell rang and Steve went to answer it. "Oh, hello, Claire, Dad." He stepped back and admitted his father and sister.

It was the first time Diana had seen Richard in weeks. She was struck by how much older he seemed. He was dressed as if for a golf outing, in tan pants and a blue polo shirt. Throughout their marriage she'd clung to the image of him as handsome and debonair, the sophisticated professor who had swept her off her feet. Now he looked like an old man, shrunken and grayer, with a receding hairline and the beginnings of a paunch.

"Sorry I'm late," Claire said as she breezed into the room. "I told Dad you wouldn't mind if he popped in for a minute." She spotted Diana and headed toward her. "Diana! You look wonderful. We brought you a present." She presented a large box topped with an oversize pink bow.

"Thank you." Diana stared at the gift, still trying to absorb the fact that her ex-husband had crashed her baby shower.

"Aren't you going to open it?" Claire said.

"Of course." Diana undid the bow, preparing herself to appear pleased, no matter what lurked within.

She removed the lid from the box to reveal an enormous pink teddy bear. The stuffed animal was easily three times the size of a newborn. The kind of thing Diana thought likely to inspire nightmares. "Isn't it adorable?" Claire squealed. "When she's older, she can sit in its lap and talk to it."

*She'll have* my *lap to sit in,* Diana thought, but managed a weak smile. "Thank you," she said. "That was very thoughtful." She handed the bear off to Margery and couldn't resist glancing at Richard. He remained by the door, looking uncomfortable, though Diana wasn't sure if the primary cause of his discomfort was seeing her again, or being with his gay son and his partner.

"Come in and have something to eat, Richard," she called. "Eric has made some marvelous food. And I'm sure if you asked, Steve would fix you a drink."

"Thank you, but I don't need a drink." He didn't budge from his spot by the door.

Claire walked over and grabbed his hand. "Daddy and I were hoping we could talk to you privately for a minute," she said.

Diana glanced at Steve. He gave a slight shake of his

head, indicating he had no idea what this was all about. "You can use the guest room," he said, nodding toward the hall that led from the living room.

Diana debated refusing. She really had no desire to talk to Richard or Claire. But if she didn't comply, Claire would continue to nag her, spoiling the party for everyone else. "All right." She rose slowly and made her way down the hall, Richard and Claire following. She was aware that she'd recently adopted the waddling walk of the very pregnant, and feared Richard was staring at her rear end, which suddenly felt enormous.

In the bedroom, Claire shut the door behind her and leaned against it. Diana shoved aside a pile of jackets and purses and settled uncomfortably on the edge of the bed. "What did you want to talk to me about?" she asked.

Richard glanced at Claire, who nodded encouragingly. He cleared his throat and addressed Diana. "You're looking well. Uh, how are you feeling?"

"I'm nine months pregnant," she said. "How do you think I'm feeling? My back hurts, my feet are swollen and I have constant indigestion." *And it's all your fault,* she wanted to add, but didn't.

He glanced at Claire again, with the desperate look of a man who would rather eat ground glass than be where he was at this moment.

"Daddy and I have been talking and we've hit on the perfect solution to your situation," Claire said. She spoke with the overly cheerful tone one might use to address an imbecile.

"You know a cure for indigestion?" Diana asked.

Claire looked confused, then gave a nervous laugh. "You always did have such a sense of humor," she said. "No, I mean, your situation. The baby."

"What about the baby?"

"Well, I mean, obviously, this wasn't a *planned* pregnancy. Who would have thought you'd have a baby at *your* age? Just when you and Daddy were looking forward to a fun retirement."

"I'm only fourteen years older than you are," Diana said. "I'm hardly ready for a wheelchair. And women giving birth in their forties is becoming more and more common."

"Well, yes." Annoyance flashed briefly across Claire's face before she covered it up with an expression of false concern. "But again, this wasn't something you planned, and I know it's upset your life greatly."

"Actually, I've really enjoyed my life these past few months," Diana said. She smiled at Richard and his daughter. If he was under some mistaken impression that she'd been pining for him, she wanted to dispel that thought immediately.

"Still, being a single mother—especially, an older single mother—is very hard," Claire persisted. "And it's not really the ideal way to raise a child."

"I certainly didn't set out to be a single mother," Diana said. At her words, Richard flinched. "But I'm perfectly happy to raise my daughter on my own. I have plenty of friends to help, and I don't think she'll miss out on anything."

"But a young mother and father who are eager to raise a child—especially a couple who are actually *related* to the child—would be a much more ideal situation," Claire said.

Diana struggled to make sense of what Claire was saying. "Are you suggesting I give up my daughter for adoption?" she asked.

"Exactly!" Claire beamed. "I knew you'd understand. It's the perfect solution."

"It's a ridiculous idea." Diana shoved herself into a standing position once more. "Why would I give my child to strangers when I'm perfectly capable of raising her myself?"

"Not strangers!" Claire protested. "I meant you should allow Derek and I to adopt her. Don't you see how perfect that would be? You'd still see her grow up and know she was safe, but you wouldn't have the burden of caring for her."

Diana stared at Claire. Had her stepdaughter really said what Diana thought she'd said? "I don't consider caring for my child to be a burden."

"Raising a child alone is *hard,* Diana," Claire said. "Surely you understand that. Whereas Derek and I could give this baby every advantage—"

"No!" The denial burst from her, propelled out in a rush of rage. "You have done some crazy, offensive things in your life, Claire, but this is too much. I am not giving my baby to you or to anyone else."

She tried to move past Claire, but Richard, who had so far allowed his daughter to do most of the talking, put out his hand to stop her. "Think about this, Di," he said. "If you gave the baby to Claire to raise, you and I could go back to the life we had. I really do miss you."

The sadness in his eyes tugged at her heart, and she searched for an easy way to let him down, to let him know she *didn't* miss him, without being cruel about it. But his next words destroyed whatever sympathy she'd been building for him.

"We'd be free to travel," he said. "I'd take you to Rome. I know you've always wanted to go to Rome."

"You think I'd trade my child in for a *vacation?*" Diana's voice rose in a shriek, but she didn't care. What had she ever seen in this man?

There was a knock on the door. "Is everything all right in there?" Steve asked.

"Claire and Richard were just leaving," Diana said loudly. This time she succeeded in pushing past them and wrenching open the door.

"Are you okay?" Steve took her arm and led her to the living room sofa. "Your face is all red. You're not in labor, are you?"

She was shaking all over, but she refused to show any weakness as long as Claire and Richard were anywhere near. "I'll be fine. Just— Make sure your sister and father leave."

"I already showed them out." Eric appeared at her elbow. He handed her a glass of sparkling water with lemon. "What did they say to you? Claire looked ready to eat nails."

"They thought it would be a wonderful idea for me

to give my baby to Claire and her husband to raise." Diana gulped water, trying to regain some semblance of calm.

"What?" Margery asked. "Why would they think that?"

"Claire would have the baby she wants and everything would be clear for Richard and I to get back together."

"Since when do you want to get back with Richard?" Margery asked.

"I don't. And I'm sorry Claire hasn't been able to have a baby of her own, but she can't have mine." The very idea sent a haze of anger across Diana's vision.

Steve shook his head. "I swear, I don't know how I'm even related to that woman," he said. "As for my father…"

"It doesn't matter. I made it clear what I thought of the idea." Now that Diana had had time to collect herself, she saw how things must have appeared to Claire and Richard: Claire always got everything she wanted from her father, so why not a baby? As for Richard, Diana had done whatever he asked of her for most of their marriage, so why should she behave any differently now?

Except she was different now. She would never go back to the peace-at-any-price wife who put her own wishes and needs second in order to placate her husband. From now on, she followed her own course for her life, and woe to any man—or woman—who tried to stop her.

## CHAPTER NINE

"WHAT'S THE LATEST on the new playscape?" Graham leaned against the doorframe to Jason's office one Tuesday afternoon two weeks after the contracts had been signed.

"The contractor has moved the old playground equipment and is pouring footings for the new equipment," Jason said. "I spoke to the foreman this morning. Why? Did you notice something wrong?"

"Only that I haven't seen the playscape's designer around lately. Shouldn't she be supervising or something?"

"I'm sure she's communicating with the contractor." Jason struggled to keep his expression noncommittal. He'd hoped to see Diana at the school before now, too. Was she avoiding him because of that kiss in his kitchen? Had he offended her with his behavior?

"You should call her," Graham said. "Ask her to come here."

"Why should I do that?" Jason eyed his friend curiously.

"Because she's a nice woman and you'd like to see her again?"

Diana *was* a nice woman. And he *would* like to see her again.

But his feelings obviously didn't matter, since Diana was clearly avoiding him. "I need to focus on getting things straightened out with Kinsey right now," he said. "I don't have time for a new relationship." Diana deserved a man who could focus all his attention and effort on her.

"What about friendship?" Graham asked. "A man can't have too many friends."

"Diana's busy getting ready for her new baby. And I'm sure she has plenty of friends already."

"Tell her you need a woman you can call on when Kinsey has questions you can't answer. Questions only a woman, a mother herself, can deal with."

"Kinsey already has a mother."

"But not one right here, where she could meet with her face-to-face."

"I don't need you to think up excuses for me to contact a woman," Jason said.

"Somebody needs to help you. You've been divorced a year now, and separated for a year before that, and as far as I know, you haven't been on a single date."

"Why would I be anxious to get back into the mess I just got out of?"

"You know what they say—if you get thrown from a horse, the best thing for it is to get right back on."

"Who is this mysterious 'they' making these pronouncements? I'm not saying I'll never date again, but I think I'm wise to be choosy."

"Choosy implies making a choice," Graham said. "I don't see you doing that."

Jason scowled at his friend. "Don't you have a class to teach?"

After Graham left, Jason stared at the phone. He missed Diana. He missed her smile and her intelligence and the way he felt more alive and aware when he was with her.

He missed having her in his life.

But he had to be careful not to send the wrong message. He didn't want her to think he was looking to date her. Which meant he'd have to take things slowly. Start casually. Let the friendship develop naturally.

As superintendent of the school, he certainly had the right to contact her. Before he could change his mind, he picked up the phone and dialed the number he'd memorized from looking at her business card so often.

"Hello?" She had the distracted sound of someone who'd been interrupted midtask.

"Diana, this is Jason Benton from Evergreen Montessori School. How are you?"

"I'm fine. How are you, Jason?" Did she sound happy to hear from him, or was that merely the polite tone she used with all her customers?

"I'm good. I called to ask if you'd stop by the school one day this week. I have some questions about the playscape."

"Is there a problem with the contractor?"

"No. He appears to be doing a good job. These are design questions I need you to answer."

Silence. Was she checking her calendar? Thinking of excuses to say no? "What are your questions?" she asked. "I might be able to answer them over the phone."

"I prefer to see you in person."

"Oh. All right. I can stop by tomorrow afternoon." She didn't sound enthusiastic about the idea, but maybe she was tired.

"Great, I'll see you then." He hung up the phone, feeling good. Now he had to come up with some questions to ask, so she wouldn't think he was wasting her time. While she was here, he'd broach the subject of the two of them staying in touch. Maybe he'd use Graham's suggestion of wanting to be able to consult her about Kinsey. That would be nonthreatening, wouldn't it?

In the meantime, maybe he'd better make an appointment for a haircut.

JASON HAD OFTEN BEEN in Diana's thoughts during the past two weeks, but work and preparations for the arrival of the baby kept her too busy to fret over him. In rare quiet moments she relived the encounter in his kitchen, and experienced again that flash of desire for him. But she wasn't the type to waste energy on regret, and told herself things had worked out as they were meant to.

But she'd deliberately stayed away from the school, using her advanced pregnancy as an excuse to allow the contractor to oversee the details of the project. She didn't trust herself to remain professionally distant in Jason's presence. He'd touched something inside her that day in the kitchen, exposing a vulnerability she hadn't known existed, and though his withdrawal had probably been wise, to that most female part of her it had felt like a rejection. She hadn't been keen to relive that feeling or, worse yet, reveal her own susceptibility to her attraction to him.

So by the time she arrived at the school the afternoon following his phone call, she was nervous and irritable. She'd been increasingly uncomfortable for the past week and was sleeping poorly. She felt fat, frumpy and in no mood to make small talk or fake a cheerful attitude. The first person who approached her the wrong way—especially if that person was a man—was liable to have his head snapped off.

As she waddled through the hallways at the school, she was aware of stares from children and adults alike. What was the matter with them? Hadn't they ever seen a woman the size of a beached whale before? Didn't they like the navy-and-white sailor dress that was almost the only thing that fit her anymore?

Jason met her at his office door, slim and polished, smelling of a mixture of woodsy cologne and starch, his gold-streaked hair neatly styled. His smile sent a flutter through her chest. Or that sensation could be indigestion.

"How have you been?" he asked, stepping forward to take her hand. "I was worried we hadn't seen you because you weren't feeling well."

"I'm fine." She slipped her hand from his. "I've just been busy. What can I do for you?"

"Let's walk out to the playground. I have some questions for you."

He led the way to the cleared area where her vision for a mountain-themed playscape was taking shape. The old equipment had been removed and sand brought in to level the surface. Footings were being poured for the large steel posts that would form the trunks of the trees that were the heart of the play structure.

"I'm concerned about the depth of the footings," Jason said. "They're only four feet deep. Shouldn't they be much deeper, considering the height of the structure?"

This was clearly something he could have asked her over the phone, but she didn't bother pointing that out. "If the posts were freestanding, the footings would need to be deeper," she said. "But since they're connected to each other and to other structures around them, there's no danger of them being blown over by high winds or weakened by repeated use. The footings are the correct depth."

"That's good to know. Now what about these slides?" He pointed to a trio of epoxy-coated metal slides—one in a spiral shape and the others straighter and undulating. "These look very steep. Are you sure they're safe?"

"They only look that steep because they're propped against a fence. They'll be perfectly safe." She glared at him, then forced herself to soften her tone. "The idea is to encourage children to have fun, not to injure or frighten them."

"Of course. I'm not questioning your intentions, I promise. I just feel a responsibility to all the children who'll be using this equipment to see that it's safe."

She nodded. On one hand, his insistence on micro-managing the project drove her nuts. He made Richard look almost laid-back and undemanding. But Jason's involvement was also part of his charm. His concern for the safety and happiness of his students was so obviously genuine.

"Do you take such a personal interest in everything that happens at the school?" she asked.

"Of course."

"You could have asked me any of this over the phone."

"I thought it would be better if we discussed it in person." He glanced at her. "Besides, I wanted to see you again."

The admission sent another flutter through her, this one centered more in her abdomen. She put a protective hand over her belly.

"Things were…awkward between us the last time we saw each other," Jason added. "I wanted to set them straight." He glanced around, as if to reassure himself they would not be overheard, then his gaze met hers. "I like you, Diana. A lot. But now isn't the time for me to start a relationship with anyone."

"I—I like you, too," she stammered. "And you're right. Now isn't a good time."

"Good." His shoulders relaxed and his smile was warmer. "When Kinsey comes to live with me, I might need the advice of a woman from time to time. I'd like to think I could call on you."

"So it's settled already? You're going to get custody?" That had happened quickly.

"No. We're still filing papers back and forth. But I'm sure living with me is the best place for her."

Diana nodded. "Of course you can call on me for help." Though did a man who was so certain of his own judgment ever really need assistance?

"One other thing, while we're here." He led the way to a shady corner of the yard. "I was thinking a jungle gym would work well here."

"A jungle gym isn't part of my design," she said.

"Yes, but the one we had was very popular with the children. I think they'd miss it."

He meant *he'd* miss it. And like Richard, he hated not getting his own way. "No jungle gym," she said firmly. She couldn't stop him from installing one after she was finished with the project, but she wouldn't compromise her design solely to please him.

He took her refusal with surprising good grace. "I couldn't pass up the opportunity to try to change your mind."

At one time, his persuasion might have worked, but she was no longer interested in smoothing things over for the sake of peace. Standing by her own decisions now felt better than giving in.

She rubbed her hand across her abdomen, trying to ease the cramping there. She'd been experiencing false labor off and on for a couple of weeks now.

Jason frowned. "Are you sure you're okay?" he asked. "You look a little pale."

"I didn't sleep well last night, that's all." She managed a smile. "I'm sure if I sit down for a moment I'll be fine."

"Of course." He ushered her inside.

In the hallway outside his office, an attractive, dark-haired woman hurried toward them. "Jason! I'm so glad I caught you in."

"Oh, hello, Beverly." He turned to Diana. "Diana, this is one of our board members, Beverly Polis. She has two children who are students here. Beverly, this is Diana Shelton, our playscape designer."

"Hello, Diana." Beverly offered her smooth, manicured hand. "My goodness, you look ready to pop. When are you due?"

"Any minute now." Diana meant the words as a joke, but she was beginning to wonder if the persistent contractions were more than false labor this time. They were stronger now, and coming closer together. Could she really be in labor?

Beverly turned her attention once more to Jason. "I'm having a few people over to my house Friday evening for drinks and dinner—some board members and other friends," she said. "I hope you can join us."

Diana was momentarily distracted from her own distress by the uncharacteristically helpless expression that flashed across Jason's face. It was the look of a cornered animal. He cleared his throat. "That's very thoughtful of you," he said. "I'll have to check my calendar."

"I already spoke with your secretary, and she says you don't have any business meetings that night. So unless you're having a rendezvous with a girlfriend I don't know about, I'm assuming you're free." She flashed a knowing smile at Diana, who had taken an unreasonable dislike to her. Maybe it was the fact that Beverly was slim, beautiful and immaculately groomed, like a sleek, dark cat with a rhinestone collar. And something about her made Diana think her invitation wasn't as innocent as it seemed.

"I'll have to get back to you," Jason said. He took Diana's elbow once more. "Right now, Diana needs a place to sit down."

"Oh, my." Beverly scrutinized Diana once more. "You don't look very well. You're not in labor, are you?"

Diana tried to swallow, but her mouth had gone dry. She winced as another wave of pain hit her. "I'm not sure," she gasped. "But, yes, I think I might be." Her eyes widened as they met Jason's. "I think I'm going to have this baby," she whispered, fear and awe warring for control.

BEVERLY SQUEALED and babbled something about ambulances and rescue squads, but Jason was too focused on Diana to pay attention to anything the other woman said. He led Diana to a chair and steadied her as she sat. "Tell me what you're feeling," he said.

"The pain's coming in sort of waves," she said. She gripped his hand hard, her eyes wide.

"Breathe deeply. I'm right here with you." He rested

his other hand on her shoulder. A deep calm had settled over him—very different from the panic he'd experienced when Candace had gone into labor. Maybe because he wasn't as emotionally invested in this baby. Or maybe because he'd been here before and knew better what to expect. "Do you want me to call an ambulance, or would you rather I drove you to the hospital in my car?" he asked.

"No ambulance." She managed a wobbly smile. "The contractions are still pretty far apart. Maybe we should just wait and see if they go away."

He laughed at the wistfulness in her voice. "I don't think they're going to go away," he said. "But we probably have plenty of time. Why don't I drive you to the hospital?"

Beverly had disappeared, but she returned now with a worried-looking Evie. "What should we do?" Evie asked. "Should I call 911?"

"That won't be necessary." He fished his keys from his pocket. "I'm going to pull my car up to the back door. Evie, wait here with Diana until I'm ready for her."

"What do you want me to do?" Beverly asked.

*Go away,* he thought. "I don't think there's anything you can do," he said. "You're free to go home now."

She looked disappointed. "Maybe I should ride with you to the hospital."

"That won't be necessary." Before she could protest, he turned and headed for the parking lot.

When he returned, Diana was less pale and frightened looking. "I called my doctor and my friend Margery, and they're both going to meet us at Swedish Hospital," she said. "Neither of them seem to think I have anything to worry about."

"Of course you don't." He helped her to stand, then put one arm around her and led her toward the back door. An unsettling sense of déjà vu washed over him as they shuffled down the hall, a memory of doing this same slow walk with Candace. She had worn that same expression of intense concentration, her focus away from him, turned inward to what was happening to her body.

With Candace, he'd felt neglected by her inattention, shut out of something he had expected to play a bigger role in. With Diana he was merely grateful to be able to offer what little help he could. It felt good to be needed, even if only as an arm to lean on and a driver to get her to the hospital.

"How are you doing?" he asked once they were settled in the car and headed downtown.

"Okay." She sounded a little breathless. Maybe she was fighting another pain.

"You don't have to be stoic with me," he said. "Cry out if it makes you feel better. I don't frighten easily." Though when Candace had let out her first moan of pain he'd felt faint.

"Giving birth doesn't allow a woman much dignity," Diana said. "Allow me to hang on to mine a little longer."

"Do you want me to put on my emergency flashers

and race toward downtown?" he asked. "If we're lucky, we'll attract the attention of a police escort."

She made a face. "Driving at a normal speed will be fine."

"Suit yourself."

"When your daughter was born, was it like this?" she asked. "Did you drive your wife to the hospital?"

"Yes. Except that Candace went into labor at two in the morning. She woke me from a sound sleep to tell me it was time, then the two of us raced around the room, throwing on clothes and bumping into each other like the Keystone Cops." He laughed at the memory of his terrified younger self. "I had had nightmares about having to deliver the baby myself, and now I was sure that was going to come true."

"And did it?"

He shook his head. "We arrived at the hospital in plenty of time. For the first half day we watched TV and talked on the phone with her mother. I'd decided it was a false alarm, and left to get a hamburger. When I got back to the hospital, her room was empty and I panicked. Turns out they'd taken her to the delivery room. I had just enough time to get changed into scrubs before my daughter was born."

"I'll bet your wife gave you a hard time about that," Diana said.

"Only a little. I told her it was her fault for waiting until I was gone to decide to get serious about having the baby."

A comfortable silence settled between them. Periodically the regular rhythm of her breathing would alter and he'd know she was having another contraction, but she gave no other sign of distress.

"I suppose I should call Richard," she said when they were near the hospital.

"Do you want him at the hospital?" Jason asked.

"No! Though I suppose as her father, he has a right to see his daughter."

"It doesn't sound as if he's shown much interest so far."

"No. He hasn't." She glanced at Jason. "Do you know what he did the other day? The day of my baby shower, in fact."

"What did he do?"

"He and Claire—I suspect it was mostly her—decided that I should let Claire adopt my baby. That way, she could have the baby she wants and I'd be free to go back to being Richard's wife without any inconvenience to him."

Jason was so startled, his foot momentarily slipped off the gas, but he quickly recovered. "What did you say when he suggested this ridiculous idea?" he asked.

"Not everything I wanted to, that's for sure. But I did let them know I thought it was a terrible idea. Frankly, I don't want either one of them coming near the baby."

"I don't see that you have any obligation to tell either one of them when she's born," Jason said. "They'll find out soon enough on their own. But keeping quiet might prevent them bothering you while you're in the hospital."

"You're right," she said. "I don't owe them anything."

They arrived and he maneuvered the car around a parked ambulance to the entrance to the emergency room. As soon as he'd helped Diana out of the car, a petite woman with a cloud of curly brown hair ran out to meet them, pushing a wheelchair. "Everything's all ready for you to check in," she said. "I filled out as much of the paperwork as I could. All you have to do is fill in the blanks and sign."

"Thank you." Diana settled into the wheelchair. "Margery, this is Jason Benton. Jason, this is my best friend, Margery Wright."

"Nice to meet you," Margery said. "And thank you for driving Diana to the hospital. She's so stubborn and independent sometimes, I was half-afraid she'd insist on trying to drive herself."

"I'd have done my best to talk her out of that."

"Thank you for everything," Diana said. "I'm in good hands now, with Margery."

That was his cue to exit gracefully, but he was reluctant to do so. Now that he was part of this little drama, he couldn't help wanting to see how it played out. "If you don't mind, I'd like to stick around for a while," he said. "Maybe meet the little girl when she makes her appearance."

Diana's smile erased the pain from her face, and made his heart feel too big for his chest. "I'd love that," she said. "I'll try not to keep you waiting too long."

"If there's one thing I've learned, it's that baby girls are worth the wait," he said. All those hours he'd spent anticipating Kinsey's arrival had meant nothing once he'd held her in his arms.

Of course, this situation wasn't the same, but he had nothing to keep him from spending a few hours in a hospital waiting room. And if this child's father wasn't interested in welcoming her to the world, there ought to be some man standing by to do so. He was happy to step in to fill that role, even if it was only temporary.

## CHAPTER TEN

ONCE DIANA WAS SETTLED into the birthing room, Margery refused to sit still. She flitted from one side of the bed to the next, peppering Diana and everyone around them with questions. "Do you want some ice chips?" she asked. "Do you need another pillow? Nurse, should we lower this bed?"

"Margery, calm down!" Diana pleaded in between the increasingly stronger labor pains. "What is wrong with you? You've done this three times before."

"Yes, but never on *this* side of the table. Before, I was too busy actually giving birth to be nervous."

Was she nervous? Diana wondered. A little anxious, maybe. In pain. But mostly impatient for all of this to be over with.

On television, everything happened so quickly. All that breathing and pushing, doctors barking orders. Real life was much more leisurely—long periods of seeming inactivity punctuated by bursts of pain and urgency.

Margery squeezed her hand as Diana fought through another contraction. "You're doing great," she said.

"It won't be much longer now," the nurse said. "I've paged the doctor."

"Did you hear that?" Margery asked, as if being in labor had suddenly rendered Diana deaf. "The doctor's on his way."

"I heard." Diana struggled to remember the breathing exercises she'd learned in class. They didn't seem to be helping that much. Maybe distraction would work. "Talk to me," she said. "About anything but the baby."

"All right." Margery looked around the room, as if searching for an appropriate topic of conversation. "I wonder if Jason is still in the waiting room?"

*Jason.* The one topic of conversation that actually could hold her attention. "I can't believe he wanted to wait," she said. "Why do you think he did that?"

"He wanted to be here to support you."

Diana waited for another pain to subside. "No... I think he just wanted to see the baby. He misses his daughter so much."

"Don't sell yourself short." Margery smiled. "I think he's here because of you. He likes you."

"And I like him." Her voice broke and she felt close to bursting into tears. It wasn't fair that she was delivering this baby on her own—well, without the baby's father. "Why couldn't someone like Jason be my baby's father?" she asked. "Instead of Richard, who doesn't even care?"

"Don't let yourself get upset this way," Margery soothed. "You're doing great. You don't need nasty old Richard or any man."

Another strong contraction prevented Diana from answering. "She's crowning," a nurse said, as the doctor walked into the door.

"You're doing terrific," the doctor said, donning fresh latex gloves. "Why don't we see about getting this baby born, shall we?"

THE WAITING ROOM for labor and delivery had the worn, neglected look of bus stations and airport gates, with the same blue upholstered chairs and gray utilitarian carpeting, and the same sense that the people here were only pausing before moving on to better things.

Jason read months-old issues of news magazines, drank weak, lukewarm coffee from the vending machine, and paced, willing himself not to check his watch every five minutes as he waited for news of Diana and her baby. He ignored the stares of the others in the room—older men and women and some younger couples, the parents and friends of parents-to-be. He was the only single man.

"I didn't think a guy could get out of being in the delivery room with his wife these days." An older man whose bald head was sprinkled with brown age spots spoke to Jason as he passed near the vending machines.

"What?" Jason halted and blinked at the man. "Oh…I'm not here with my wife," he said. "That is, I don't have a wife. I—I'm waiting for a friend."

The old guy appeared as if he didn't believe Jason. "My mistake. But you look every bit as nervous as any father I've seen." He sighed and glanced around the room. "In my day, the men huddled out here together while the women did the work. All we had to do was show up when it was over with flowers and cigars."

"Who are you waiting for?" Jason asked.

"My daughter. Her third. The baby should be here any minute now. Melissa's a real pro at this by now." He jerked his head toward the doors leading to the birthing rooms. "How long has your friend been in there?"

Jason looked at his watch. "Six hours." That long? He'd lost track of the time. "It's her first, so I guess it could be a while."

"My advice is, go get something to eat and come back later," the old man said. "These things take time."

Jason shook his head. He wouldn't make that mistake again. "No. I'm fine."

The old man moved away and Jason resumed pacing. He hoped Diana was fine. What if she wasn't? What if something happened and he'd never have a chance to tell her how much he'd enjoyed being with her—how much he'd grown to care for her?

He pushed the thought away. Nothing was going to happen to her. She'd deliver a healthy baby girl and everyone would be fine.

And then what? Could the two of them be just friends? After the kisses they'd shared and the emotional connection between them that was impossible to deny? Was he a fool to even try to keep her at a distance when all he wanted was for them to be close?

All his life, he'd struggled to do the right thing. After his father suffered a debilitating accident when Jason was twelve, Jason had wanted nothing more than for his family to be whole again. In his professional life, he'd always tried to make things perfect for his students. Then he'd married Candace and fathered Kinsey. He felt as if he'd been given a second chance to have the family he'd always wanted. He'd tried to make things right for them, but nothing had worked out the way he'd planned.

Now here he was, single and trying to piece together his life once more. The problem was, he'd spent so much time taking care of others, he wasn't sure he knew how to do the right thing for himself anymore.

DIANA HAD NEVER HEARD a sound more wonderful than the first hearty wail of her daughter. "She's beautiful!" Margery cried, and Diana raised her head, trying to see. She caught a glimpse of a tiny form surrounded by doctors and nurses.

Then someone laid the baby on her chest. "You have a beautiful baby girl," the doctor announced.

Diana stroked the tiny limbs and marveled at the damp, dark hair above the reddened face and blinking eyes. "Welcome to the world, Leah," she whispered, tears of joy streaming down her face.

"Leah? Is that her name?" Margery's voice was faint in Diana's ear and growing more distant. Still holding her daughter close, she drifted into a deep, satisfying sleep.

WHEN DIANA WOKE AGAIN, she had been moved to a room and dressed in a clean nightgown. A large arrangement of pink roses sat on a nearby table beside the bed. "The flowers are from Steve and Eric," Margery said, coming to stand beside the bed. "How are you feeling?"

Diana assessed her condition. "A little sore. A little tired still. Happy." She smiled in the direction of the incubator, where she could just make out the squirming figure of her daughter, dressed in a pink onesie and diaper, pink knit cap and booties. Diana struggled to sit up on the side of the bed. "I want to see her," she said.

"Sure thing. But let me hold on, in case you're a little unsteady on your feet."

With Margery's help, Diana shuffled over to the incubator, where she stood staring down at her daughter. Most of the redness had faded, revealing creamy skin and a tiny rosebud of a mouth. Dark curls crowned her head. "She's beautiful, isn't she?" Diana said.

"She's perfect." Margery squeezed her shoulder. "Did I hear you right in the delivery room? Did you say her name is Leah?"

Diana nodded. "Yes. Leah Carleen Shelton."

"Before I forget, your mother called while you were asleep."

"She did?" Diana was surprised—and pleased. "What did she say?"

"She said to send a picture when you get one, and she hopes the baby looks like her side of the family and not your father's. And that she'd send a gift, but she knows you probably don't need anything."

"Did she mention coming to visit?" Surely her mother would want to see her only grandchild.

"No." Margery patted her shoulder. "I'm sorry, hon. Maybe something's come up and she can't get away."

"Yes, I'm sure there are all kinds of pressing things going on at the commune." Diana shook her head. "It's all right. I'm used to it by now." Used to it, but the rejection still hurt, not only for herself, but on behalf of her daughter.

The door to the room opened and a smiling African-American woman in purple scrubs entered. "Ms. Shelton? I'm Anita Williamson, your lactation consultant," she said, offering her hand.

Diana shook hands. "You're here to teach me how to breast-feed?" she asked.

Anita laughed. "Not so much teach as offer pointers and answer any questions you might have." She looked at the incubator. "What a sweet baby. Why don't you get back in bed and get comfortable and I'll bring her to you."

Diana had read all the books and seen a short film as part of her childbirth classes, but the reality of her baby at her breast was a little daunting at first. It didn't help that Margery insisted on taking pictures. "None of your private bits are showing, I promise," she said. "You'll want these for your baby book."

Right. If the baby book was anything like other personal projects that required being organized, it would end up being a baby shoe box, stuffed full of photographs and papers in no particular order. Then again, maybe Margery, as Leah's godmother, would keep a baby book for her.

"Enough with the photographs," Anita said. "Mother and baby have work to do here." Margery put away her camera, and with coaxing from both Anita and Diana, Leah had her first feeding with a minimum of frustration on both their parts. Anita was patient and supportive, and reassured Diana she'd get the hang of it.

"I'm leaving you with some reading material and my phone number," she said at the end of forty-five minutes. "Feel free to call me any time day or night if you have questions or concerns."

When she had left, Diana settled back on the pillows, Leah sleeping peacefully in her arms. She had almost drifted off herself when there was a tap on the door and it opened slightly. "May I come in?" asked a masculine voice.

Diana blinked sleepily and sat up straighter, cradling Leah close. "Come in," she said.

Jason stuck his head around the door, and the rest of him followed, carrying a vase filled with daisies, carnations and baby's breath. "I thought you might like these," he said, with the sheepish expression of a man who wasn't sure he'd done the right thing or not.

"How thoughtful!" Margery took the flowers from him. "Diana, aren't they beautiful?"

"They are," she said. The sweetness—and the unexpectedness—of the gesture touched her. "Come over here and meet baby Leah," she said.

"How are you doing?" he asked, as he approached the side of the bed.

"I'm fine." She folded back the blanket to reveal Leah's sleeping face.

"She's beautiful," he said. Then again, what else would someone say when confronted with a newborn? Even a homely infant would elicit such praise from anyone who didn't want to incur the wrath of the mother.

"Would you like to hold her?"

He hesitated, then nodded. "Yes. Yes, I would."

She transferred the baby to his arms, aware of the intimacy of the gesture, the brush of his hand very near her breast, the catch of his breath as he cradled the tiny head and fit the swaddled infant into the crook of his arm. He straightened, his gaze fixed on the child with such tenderness Diana felt a knot of emotion in her throat.

She swallowed hard, half-fearful she'd burst into tears, and felt the tug of some primal attraction deep within her. She tried to look away, but her eyes were continually drawn to the sight of man and baby together. He smiled and stroked the infant's cheek with one finger. "You're such a pretty girl," he murmured, so softly Diana almost couldn't make out the words. "Just like your mama."

She swallowed hard, fighting against a wave of emotion that threatened to pull her under. She told herself her feelings meant nothing. What woman wouldn't be swayed by the iconic image of a strong, handsome man cradling a newborn so tenderly? Especially if the newborn was her own? Things were no doubt supposed to work that way, ensuring the bond between man and woman over the child they had created.

Except Jason wasn't this baby's father, she reminded herself. She had no need to bond with him.

"You're a natural with that baby," Margery said.

"I have a daughter of my own." He rocked Leah gently in his arms. "She's almost seven now, but this sure brings back memories."

Was he aware that he was making memories Diana wouldn't soon forget?

"I have to get a picture of this," Margery said. She snapped off several photos of Jason with Leah, then checked the display on her digital camera. "Oh, these came out nice."

Leah began to fuss, making unhappy, mewling sounds. "I'd better turn her back over to Mama," Jason said, and transferred her into Diana's arms once more.

Their eyes met over the top of the child's head and Diana felt the impact of a connection she was reluctant to investigate further.

"I'd better go and let you get some rest," he said, though his eyes remained fixed on her, as if he was reluctant to leave.

"Thank you for everything," she said. "For driving me and for the flowers…and for staying to see the baby. I really appreciate it."

"It was my pleasure." He looked at her a moment longer, then moved toward the door. "Congratulations. She's a beautiful baby." Then he slipped out as quietly as he'd arrived.

"Well," Margery said after a few seconds. "You didn't tell me he was so good-looking."

"I'm sure I did." Diana shifted the baby to her other arm. Looks weren't everything. Though if she was honest with herself, it had never been Jason's looks that had attracted her, so much as his gentle demeanor and quiet strength.

"Did you see him with Leah? No hesitation or nervousness at all. She seemed right at home there in his arms."

"He told you he has a daughter. And he's the superintendent of a school. He's used to being around children."

Margery settled into a chair beside the bed. "He didn't spend the last ten hours waiting to see you because he likes children," she said.

Diana flushed. Had Jason really waited that long? She'd lost track of the time. "He was being polite." Though she couldn't make herself believe good manners really had anything to do with it. Jason had stayed to see her and her baby. But why? "He misses his little girl," she said. "She's living in France with her mother. Maybe he wanted to remember her birth, when things were better."

"That could be part of it," Margery conceded. "But I saw the way he looked at you, too."

"He didn't look at me any special way."

"Yes, he did." Margery nudged her. "You looked pretty interested in him, too."

"What woman isn't going to get all mushy about a hot guy holding a baby?" Diana said. "It doesn't mean I'm in love with him or anything."

"Who said anything about love? *I* certainly didn't bring it up." Margery grinned. "But now that you mention it, what kind of man spends all that time sitting in those hard plastic waiting room chairs if he isn't in love?"

Diana stomach was suddenly full of butterflies. "Margery, please. Don't make more of this than it is."

"More than you want it to be, you mean." Margery's expression sobered. "I know you, Little Miss Independent. You shed yourself of one husband and you're not anxious to saddle yourself with another one. I understand that. But remember, not all men are like Richard. There are some good ones out there. Jason might be one of them."

"He's all wrong for me," Diana said, her tone pleading.

"How do you figure that? He's good-looking, gainfully employed and he loves kids."

"He's also a nitpicky micromanager who's used to getting his own way," she said. "You should see his house—a place for everything and everything in its place. And not a speck of dust."

"You've been in his house? When?"

"I took some contracts by to sign. The point is, I'm disorganized and creative and I hate anyone telling me what to do. I had my fill of that with Richard."

"So you work around your personality differences. That's what makes life interesting."

"I'm done with interesting. All I want now is to be left alone to raise my daughter as I see fit."

"I do believe I'm entitled to some say in how she's brought up."

Both women turned and saw Richard in the doorway. Margery stood and moved to one side, as if poised to run for help. Diana looked past him, expecting to see Claire also, but he was alone. "Richard, what are you doing here?" she asked.

"I came to see my daughter." He moved into the room and studied the swaddled infant in Diana's arms. "Steven told me she'd been born. I assume she has the correct number of arms and legs and fingers and toes?"

Diana held the baby closer. "She's beautiful and perfectly healthy."

"Then may I see her?"

Reluctantly, she loosened her hold on the child and folded back the blankets so that Richard could see her. "Her name is Leah," she said, daring him to argue with her choice.

"I had an aunt named Leah," he said, nodding.

"I didn't name her after your aunt. I named her because I like the name."

Without being asked, he settled into the chair Margery had vacated. Margery stood by the door. "Do you want me to leave?" she asked.

"Yes," Richard said.

"Why don't you go get some coffee?" Diana said. "Come back in a few minutes."

"I won't be far. Try not to upset her, Richard."

"I'm not upsetting anyone. I'm merely sitting here."

He said nothing further, even after they were alone. The only sounds were the ticking of the bedside clock and Leah's soft mouth sounds. The silence stretched tight, until Diana's nerves were frayed. "I thought Claire would be with you," she said at last.

"Claire is very upset with you," he said. "She was genuinely trying to help you, and you hurt her feelings."

The words were like a match to Diana's anger. "Did she really expect me to see her wanting to take my baby as a *favor?*" Her voice rose and Leah began to cry. Diana glared at Richard.

He didn't react, merely sat in the chair, watching her. "You look very comfortable," he said. "Very…natural, holding a child."

"Richard, why are you here? You've made it clear ever since I told you about my pregnancy that you wanted nothing to do with this baby or with me if I insisted on having her."

He let out a heavy sigh. "I came to try to explain," he said. "I know you think I'm a horrible person, but what's so horrible about a person who acknowledges his shortcomings and does his best not to inflict them on others?"

Since when had Richard ever refrained from inflicting himself on others? The man lived to give orders and to force others to do his will. "Which shortcomings in particular?" she asked.

His frown deepened. "I made it clear from the beginning of our relationship that I was not comfortable with children. I don't enjoy their company. I know I have not been a good father to the three I already have. Claire is highstrung and spoiled. Marcus has distanced himself from me altogether, and Steven…" His voice trailed away.

"Steven is gay. And happy in a committed relationship. In spite of your parenting, or lack thereof."

"The point is, fatherhood is not something I'm good at, so I had no wish to repeat the experience. Especially at a time in my life when I was very settled and happy." His eyes met hers—eyes as familiar to her as her own, after eighteen years of looking at them across the dinner table each night. "When *we* were happy," he said.

She shook her head. "You were happy," she said. "You thought I was happy. Maybe *I* even thought I was happy. But the truth was I hadn't been happy for years."

He looked surprised. "Because I refused to have more children?"

"That was part of it. But mostly, I was unhappy because I was trying to be someone I was not. You wanted a wife who would cater to you, someone more…passive, who would allow you to make all the decisions, to take care of her. When we first married, I thought I could be that kind of woman, but I found out I couldn't."

"I'm sorry to hear that." He fell silent again, though the tension between them was gone now, replaced by a heavy sadness. "I don't think it makes me a bad person to wish things could go back to the way they were," he said.

"But they never can." She smoothed a wisp of dark hair across Leah's forehead. "I know you didn't ask to be a father at this stage of your life," she said. "I'd like it if you chose to have a relationship with your daughter, but if you're not capable of that, I won't force the issue. It's your decision. Leah and I will be just fine on our own."

"I'm sure you will." He stood and moved toward the door. "But I wonder if you won't be lonely, too."

He left, shutting the door firmly behind him, his last words echoing in her head. He didn't know lonely. Lonely was living in a marriage where you felt more like an extension of someone else than an individual.

Lonely wasn't the same as being alone. In these past few months, she'd discovered the pleasure of her own company. And now she had Leah. Surely she didn't need anything more.

## CHAPTER ELEVEN

HOLDING DIANA'S BABY had filled Jason with memories of his own daughter's birth. In those early days, Kinsey had been colicky, and it had taken everything both parents had to care for her. Jason had spent many long nights walking the floor with the child in his arms, talking to her about every subject under the sun, distracting them both from her bouts of crying.

He would have given anything to experience even those miserable nights again.

When he arrived home from the hospital that evening his house seemed even colder and darker than usual. After a shower and a ham sandwich he crawled into bed, but was unable to sleep. It was after midnight in Colorado, which meant it was just past eight in the morning in Paris. He ought to be able to catch Kinsey before she left for school. If he could talk to her for a few minutes, he knew he'd feel better.

"Allô?" Candace's voice, so lyrical and sweet, caught him off guard. Usually when he called, Kinsey answered the phone. But those calls were always prearranged.

*"Allô. Qui s'appelle?"*

"Candace, this is Jason. May I speak to Kinsey?"

"Jason? Why on earth are you calling at his hour? Is something wrong?"

"Nothing's wrong. I just wanted to speak to Kinsey before she left for school."

"I don't know if that's a good idea. She's always so upset after she talks to you, and I don't want her starting her day that way."

"If she's upset, it's because she misses me."

"Of course she misses you, but that's not what upsets her. It's because you make her feel guilty about being here with me. That's a terrible burden to place on a seven-year-old."

"I don't *make* her feel guilty," he protested. "I know she had nothing to do with your decision to take her away."

"You make it sound as if I deliberately set out to marry a man who worked in France, in order to spite you."

Could he help it if he sometimes felt that was exactly what she'd done? Not choosing a man from France so much as working to put as much distance as possible between him and her and their daughter. "Let me speak to Kinsey," he said.

"Only if you promise to try to sound happy."

"Happy about being apart from her? I could never do that."

"She's a child, Jason. She doesn't need to be burdened with your unhappiness. I'm sorry you're sad and lonely, but it would be much easier on everyone if you'd get on with your life and stop trying to get things back to the way they were. They're never going to be that way and you'd be much healthier and, I hope, happier, if you'd start dating, maybe marry again and even have another family."

"Kinsey is my daughter. You can't ask me to forget about her."

"Of course I'm not asking you to forget about her. You'll always be an important part of her life. But she'd be happier if she knew you were doing all right without her there by your side. That she could live her own life without worrying so much about you."

As if Candace knew what was best for him and his daughter. "Let me talk to her," he said again, the words squeezed out through clenched teeth.

A few seconds later, Kinsey came on the line. "Hi, Daddy. You're up early," she said.

"Actually, it's very late here," he said. "After midnight. I was getting ready to go to bed and was thinking about you, so I thought I'd call."

"That's good. But I can't talk long. Victor is waiting to drive me to school."

"Why doesn't your mother take you?"

"She's busy working, while the morning light is so good. Besides, Victor goes right past my school on his way to the coffee shop where he meets with his agent and other actors."

Jason pictured the Frenchman lazing the day away at a coffee shop while Candace lost all track of time, absorbed in her paintings. No one cleaned the house, no one prepared regular meals. What kind of environment was that for a young girl to grow up in?

"Are you okay, Daddy?" she asked. "Is something wrong? You don't usually call so early."

"I'm fine." His voice cracked, and he cleared his throat. "I just wanted to ask you a question," he said.

"What is it?"

"Are you happy? I mean, living there with your mom and Victor? Do you like it?"

There was a long silence, so long he wondered if they'd lost their connection. "You know I miss you," she said finally.

"This isn't about me," he said. "I'm fine. I want to know if you're happy. If you are, that's all that matters."

"I *do* like it here," she said. "I didn't at first, because I didn't know anyone. But it's different now. I have friends and my teacher says my French is improving every day." She lowered her voice. "And I've got a secret, but you must promise not to tell anyone."

"I promise," he said solemnly, hoping she wasn't going to tell him she had a boyfriend.

"I'm going to have a little brother or sister soon."

What was she talking about? "Is this something at school, where they pair you with a younger child?" he asked.

She laughed. She had her mother's musical laugh. "No, silly! Maman is going to have a baby. She let me feel the little bump on her tummy and she told me the baby was inside there, growing until it's big enough to come out."

Jason felt dizzy and realized he'd stopped breathing. He sucked in a deep breath and tried to collect his thoughts. "Your mother is pregnant?" he asked.

"Yes. And Victor is so excited. He said I can help him buy the furniture for the baby's room, and I can decide what color to paint it."

"You sound excited about it."

"Oh, I am. I can't wait to be a big sister. Maman says I can help look after the baby. She's going to get me a life-size doll and teach me how to diaper it and hold it properly and everything."

"That's great." He cleared his throat. "You'll make a wonderful big sister."

"The baby won't be here yet when I come to see you this summer, but you can meet him or her the next time you visit us in Paris."

"Yeah, that'd be great."

"I have to go now, Daddy. Goodbye."

"Goodbye, sweet pea. I love you." But the dial tone drowned out these last words.

Heart pounding, he sat back against the pillows piled at the head of his bed. Candace was pregnant? Kinsey sounded thrilled at the idea, but how happy would she be once the baby arrived and Kinsey got even less of Candace's attention? Would she think Jason was doing her a favor, bringing her to live with him and be the center of his world? Or would she resent him for taking her away from her happy Parisian family?

He rubbed his pounding temples and shut his eyes, which felt lined with grit. Candace's charge that he was hurting Kinsey by making her feel guilty stung. He'd never blamed Kinsey for anything that happened, and hated she'd somehow drawn that conclusion. When he'd told her he missed her it had been his way of letting her know how much he cared. How much he wanted to be with her.

Instead, apparently she felt sorry for him. And in Candace's eyes, at least, he was a pathetic excuse for a man who was wallowing in the past, refusing to move on with his life.

She made it sound as if he wasn't able to make it without her. Yes, he missed Kinsey, but that didn't mean he'd stopped living. He enjoyed his job and he had plenty of friends—old ones like Graham and Mitch, and new ones like Diana.

So what if he hadn't rushed right into a new romantic relationship? He didn't share Candace's impulsive nature when it came to something as serious as love. There were a great many factors to consider, such as compatibility and personality traits and goals for the future.

He'd allowed emotion to guide him in his first marriage, and the results had been disastrous, not only for him, but for his child. Next time he allowed himself to fall in love he'd make sure he was guided by his head and not only his heart.

BY HER THIRD DAY home with the baby, Diana was feeling a little overwhelmed. Every waking moment was devoted to the infant in her care; her daughter's life was literally in her hands and the responsibility was daunting. Little and big tasks—from feeding to changing her baby, from establishing sleep routines to selecting lullabies—all fell on Diana's shoulders and at times it seemed like too much. After all the flowers and visits from well-wishers at the hospital, she was a little let down and lonely, too. Baxter, Claire's dog, did his best to keep her company. Apparently, Claire had forgotten all about the little animal, and Diana was reluctant to broach the subject and have her take the dog back. She'd grown to love Baxter, more than Claire ever would, Diana was sure. She welcomed the small brown bundle that curled beside her in bed each night, even if it wasn't the same as having another adult to talk to.

So when the doorbell rang after she'd put Leah to sleep, she welcomed the interruption. Maybe it was Margery, stopping by with a homemade casserole and plenty of reassurance that Diana was not going to ruin her daughter's life if she made a wrong decision.

"Hello, Diana. I thought it was time I stopped by and met my new little sister." Claire strolled in as if she wasn't the last person Diana expected to see. Dressed in black flared pants, an embroidered silk tunic and stilettos, Claire looked as if she could have come from a Junior League meeting or a two-martini lunch at some trendy downtown bistro.

"I thought you weren't speaking to me," Diana said, following Claire into the room.

"Where would you get an idea like that?"

Steve had told her, but Diana kept this information

to herself. "You weren't very happy with me the last time we spoke," she said.

"Oh, that." Claire dismissed the whole episode with a wave of her hand. "Where is the baby? I want to see her."

"I just put her down for her nap." Diana was torn between wanting to show off her child and protecting the infant—and herself—from any claims Claire might make on her.

Apparently awakened from his own nap, Baxter scampered into the room, barking excitedly and wagging his tail. He danced around Claire, who frowned down at him.

"He's happy to see you," Diana said.

"I suppose I should have come and gotten him from you before now," Claire said. "But I've been so busy. I guess I'll take him to the shelter and see if they can find a home for him. I have too much to do to look after him properly."

"Don't do that!" Diana called the little dog over to her and smoothed his curly coat. "I'll keep him. He's good company for me, and no trouble at all." She wanted to berate Claire for adopting the dog, then discarding it so thoughtlessly, but there was no sense arguing over the matter. And Diana knew Baxter would have a better home with her.

"All right. If you don't think he's too much trouble with a baby."

"Not at all. I'd love to have him."

"Now I want to see the baby." Claire headed down the hall and Diana hurried after her.

When Diana reached the nursery, Claire was already standing by the crib. Her normally cool expression was all softness and warmth as she gazed at the infant, who stared up at her with solemn eyes. "Isn't she beautiful?" Claire said. Before Diana could stop her, she bent and scooped the baby into her arms.

Diana flinched, and had to fight to keep from reaching out and snatching the baby away. It wasn't as if Claire would kidnap Leah with Diana right there, though after that confrontation at the baby shower, Diana could never completely trust her stepdaughter again.

"Aren't you precious?" Claire cooed, rocking Leah gently in her arms. "I'm Claire, your big sister. You and I are going to have lots of fun times together."

Diana somehow refrained from contradicting this. Claire was definitely not the role model she wanted for her daughter. "Let's go into the other room and sit down," she said. "I was about to make some tea. Would you like some?"

"All right." Still focused on the baby in her arms, she followed Diana and Baxter into the kitchen, where she sat at the table while Diana filled the kettle and set it on the stove. "Steve said you'd named her Leah," Claire said. "Is that a family name or something?"

"No, I just like the name. I think it suits her."

Claire studied the baby once more. "She looks like pictures of me when I was a baby."

Diana's hands shook as she took two mugs from a rack by the sink. "I think she looks like herself," she said quietly.

"Yes, but there's a definite family resemblance. If we went out together, I bet people would think she's my daughter."

Diana turned to face Claire, holding on to the counter to keep from flying at the younger woman. "Claire, look at me," she commanded.

Claire raised her head expectantly. "Yes?"

"Leah is not your baby. She will never be your baby. I am not going to give her up to you or to anyone else. Is that clear?"

Her expression clouded. "Of course I understand," she said stiffly. "I'm not an imbecile. I was only saying we looked like each other." To Diana's dismay, her lower lip began to tremble. "But it's not fair that you should have such a beautiful baby when I can't have one at all."

This was a familiar pattern, Diana thought as she rushed to Claire's side. How many times had she soothed and tried to comfort her stepdaughter whenever she wailed that life was being terribly unfair? Claire might be a grown woman, but to Diana, the hurting little girl inside of her was so clear. "You're very young still," she said, patting Claire's shoulder. "You have time. And you're well off financially. You can pursue medical treatments, or you could adopt. You have plenty of options."

Claire sniffed and dabbed at her eyes with the tissue Diana handed her. "The funny thing is, I didn't even *want* children until you got pregnant," she said. "Then, all of a sudden, I knew I wanted a family of my own. I know I could be a good mother. And Derek will make a wonderful father. He'll be involved in his children's lives, always there for them."

*Unlike Richard,* Diana thought. "What does your doctor say?" she asked.

"He says it's too soon to panic—that we should relax and be patient."

"That sounds like good advice."

"I'm tired of people telling me to be patient!" Claire's vehemence caught Diana off guard. "Why should I have to wait for what I want when other people certainly don't?"

"Claire, people have to wait all the time for what they want."

"You certainly didn't. You didn't even give Daddy a chance when you decided to have this baby. You went running off on your own without a look back."

"Is that what he told you?"

"He didn't have to tell me." Claire stuck her chin in the air. "I know how you are. Did you even consider that finding out he was going to be a father at fifty-five was a shock to him? That he might have said things he didn't mean in the heat of the moment? If you'd given him a chance, if you'd been *patient,* I'm sure he would have changed his mind."

"You're sure of that?" Diana asked. Was Claire really so blind to her father's faults?

"Of course I'm sure." Her expression softened as she looked at Leah. "How could he not love a beautiful baby girl like this?"

Understanding dawned as Diana recognized the fear behind Claire's words. If Richard really didn't love and want his new daughter, maybe that meant he'd never wanted and loved the old one, either. "Claire, your father's feelings for you are separate from his feelings—whatever they are—for Leah," she said. "As you said, he's older now, at a different place in his life. Whatever you believe, I didn't see a way to have your father and Leah."

She took the baby from Claire and cradled the infant close. "One day maybe you'll understand why I made the choice I did."

"I'll never understand you." Claire stood and straightened her clothes. "Not that you've made much effort to understand me."

"That's not true." Diana had spent many sleepless nights and anxious days during Claire's teen years attempting to figure out why her stepdaughter behaved the way she did.

"I know what you think of me," Claire said. "You think I'm spoiled. Difficult. But you don't know how it was, living in your shadow all these years. No matter what I tried to do, you did it first or better."

"What are you talking about?" Diana asked, truly puzzled.

"Don't you remember? The Christmas I worked so hard, saving my money to buy Daddy a watch for Christmas. You gave him a gold money clip that made my watch look cheap. And the year I was in the homecoming court of honor, *you* volunteered to be in charge of the after-party. All I heard about all evening was how great the decorations and the food were. Then my date even asked you to dance. I was mortified."

Diana listened to this recitation of her sins—most of which she'd forgotten—stunned.

"You've spent my whole life trying to upstage me," Claire continued. "And now you had to go and have a baby before I did. At your age! Can't you see how unbearable this is?"

Not waiting for an answer, she fled. Diana sank into the chair Claire had vacated and listened to the front door slam, the rev of the car engine and the squeal of tires as Claire drove away. Diana had devoted so many years to trying to be a good mother to her stepchildren, but all Claire could see her as was competition.

Baxter sat at Diana's feet and whined. She scratched behind his ears. "Looks like you're my dog now," she said. "You're happy about that, aren't you? I'll be a much better doggy mom than she was."

Baxter wagged the stump of his tail and licked the back of Diana's hand.

Leah began to fuss and Diana unbuttoned her blouse and encouraged the baby to nurse. She was still trying to get the hang of breast-feeding, but she and Leah were muddling along together. She hoped they would always be close like this. She wanted her daughter to know all the love and security she'd only dreamed about as a child herself.

Not that her parents didn't love her. But they'd been young—only seventeen and eighteen—when Diana was born. They both changed jobs frequently and there was never a lot of money. They preferred partying with their friends to staying home with a baby, and even at the young age of nine years old, Diana had been left alone for long hours to fend for herself. She'd spent many of those hours imagining a different kind of life— one filled with comfort and security, and most of all, love.

More than anything, Diana had wanted to give Richard's children the happy, loving childhood she herself had never had. But while the boys had warmed to her almost immediately, Claire had resisted every effort to draw her close.

"I guess that's the thing," she said out loud to Leah and the dog. "You can't make someone love you. And sometimes I guess you have to know when to stop trying."

HALF A DOZEN TIMES in the days after he left her at the hospital, Jason picked up the phone to call Diana, but he always backed down. He told himself the timing wasn't right; they each had too many other things going on. But he knew what held him back was plain old fear—fear of making the same kind of mistake he'd made with Candace. Fear of screwing up his own life and that of a child by getting involved with someone who was all wrong for him, no matter how strong their physical attraction.

All this logical thinking hadn't prepared him for his reaction when Diana walked into his office one afternoon four weeks after her baby was born. He blinked, trying hard not to stare. The pretty mother-to-be had been replaced by a slim, chic siren in a bright red suit and heels. If not for the baby carried in a shawl wrapped close around her body, he might not have believed she'd recently given birth.

"Hello, Jason," she said, jolting him from his stupor.

"This is a pleasant surprise," he said, standing and moving around his desk to meet her. "How are you doing?"

She took the chair he offered and adjusted the shawl to reveal the sleeping infant. "I'm doing great." Her smile hit him with the force of a laser, full of sass and sex appeal. She might be a new mother, yet she was anything but matronly.

Determined to regain control of his emotions, he leaned over her to admire the baby, catching the mingled scents of baby powder and herbal shampoo. In an instant he was catapulted back to the kiss they had shared, that moment of intense intimacy that still shook him whenever he thought about it.

"Say hello to Jason, Leah," Diana cooed.

He stroked Leah's tiny hand and she grasped his finger with a surprisingly strong grip. It felt as if she was tugging directly on his heart. He straightened, needing to put a little distance between himself and them, to get a better hold on his emotions. "She looks as if she's grown," he said.

"She's doing great."

"Do you have all the help you need with her?" He

had vivid memories of how exhausted both he and Candace had been in those early months with Kinsey. Yet Diana looked fresh and even well-rested.

"I've had plenty of offers of help, but I've been managing fine on my own." She tucked the shawl more securely around the baby. "She and I have a routine down now, so everything's going pretty smoothly."

He didn't miss the note of pride in her voice. Of course she didn't need anyone to help her with her daughter. She was too independent to need anyone else in her life. "What brings you here today?" he asked.

"I was going stir-crazy sitting around the house, so I thought it was time I got back to work."

"With the baby along?"

"Why not? She's easy enough to look after. Margery has offered to babysit, but right now it's easier for me to have her with me."

"Of course." A little unconventional, maybe, but she wouldn't care about that, would she?

"Let's go out and see how the construction is coming." She stood and led the way to the door.

He followed, unable to stop watching the gentle sway of her hips. So much for business-as-usual. The woman had walked into his office and awakened every dormant desire he'd held at bay for the past year.

"It's looking wonderful," she said as she surveyed the almost completed playscape. All the structures were in place, though finishing, painting and landscaping had yet to be done. Metal tree trunks and branches towered over attached swings and slides, and a vertical sheet of wood awaited the fake rocks that would transform it into a climbing wall. "Are the children excited?" she asked.

"They are," he said. "Every day half a dozen of them ask me when it's going to be ready for them."

"A couple of weeks now, I think," she said. She walked around one of the tree trunks and gazed up at the platform overhead. "They're going to have a lot of fun with this."

"What's the next step?" he asked.

"The painting," she said. "That's one of the reasons I stopped by. I want to check the colors. The contractor promised to leave me some samples." She scanned the underside of the structure, then pointed to a section of the metal that had been painted in stripes of different colors. "There they are. What do you think?"

Jason stared at the bright blue, purple and green swaths of paint with dismay. "They're so bright," he said. If small sections of paint were this bold, he could only imagine how eye-popping the finished structure would be.

"Children like bright colors," she said. "They're stimulating."

"Yes, I know that. But I thought we agreed the colors would be more subdued. In keeping with the surroundings."

"I took out the yellow and orange." She stepped back and looked up at the structure. "Trust me. It's going to be beautiful."

*You're beautiful.* The words came unbidden, though he couldn't say them out loud. He wanted to be firm and insist she change the paint colors, but he was entranced by this slender, energetic version of her. His gaze kept shifting to take in the soft curves of full breasts and trim waist. She practically glowed with vivacity and happiness.

"Why are you looking at me like that?" she asked.

He started. "I wasn't looking at you any particular way," he lied, carefully focusing on the ramp of a slide.

"Don't try to lie to me," she said, eyes sparkling, her tone light and teasing. "I know how much you hate when anyone disagrees with your ideas. You're as set in your ways as my old grandpa."

He drew himself up to his full height. "I am definitely not your old grandpa." He certainly wasn't having grandfatherly thoughts about her right now. He was thinking how much he'd like to pull her into the shadows beneath the playscape and kiss her until they were both breathless.

Their eyes met and her smile vanished, replaced by a smoldering look that made him wonder if she was thinking about kisses also.

"Ms. Shelton?"

They both looked up as Evie stepped into the yard. "There's someone here to see you," she said.

"To see me?" Diana asked.

"Yes. She says she's a friend of yours."

DIANA COULDN'T IMAGINE who would have tracked her down at the school. Had Claire seen her car out front and come in to confront her about some slight, real or imagined?

In any case, it was just as well someone had interrupted her and Jason. The last look he'd given her had been enough to melt any resolve she'd had to keep things strictly professional between them. It had taken all her willpower not to grab him by the tie and drag him to some dark corner to verify the one kiss they'd shared had been as amazing as she remembered.

"I hope I wasn't interrupting anything," Margery said, emerging from the office and coming down the hall to meet them.

"Margery, what are you doing here?" Diana's heart pounded. "Is something wrong? One of the children?"

"No, no, no! Nothing's wrong." Margery took both her hands and squeezed them reassuringly. "I didn't mean to alarm you. I only stopped by to ask you for a favor."

"A favor?" Diana eyed her friend with growing suspicion. She and Margery had talked on the phone only a couple of hours before. Diane had shared her plans to visit the school—and Jason—that afternoon. If Margery had needed a favor, why hadn't she asked about it then?

"Hello, Jason." Margery smiled and offered her hand. "You're looking a little more rested than last time we met."

"Hello again." Jason shook her hand. "It's good to see you."

"Isn't our girl looking beautiful?" Margery beamed at Diana; was she talking about the baby, or Diana herself?

"What's the favor?" Diana asked.

"Jack made reservations for tonight at that wonderful new bistro on the 16th Street Mall downtown,"

Margery said. "But something's come up at work and now he can't go. The place is so difficult to get a table at, I hated to cancel without offering them to you first."

"To me?"

"To you and Jason." Margery looked inordinately pleased with herself. "You're long overdue for a nice dinner out," she said. "I could watch Leah and you could enjoy yourselves."

"Margery!" Diana's face burned. Her friend had done a lot of things for her over the years, but this was going too far. She didn't dare glance at Jason. She hoped he didn't think she was so desperate she'd put Margery up to this. As if she needed someone else's help getting a date.

"I think that's a wonderful idea," he said. "What time is the reservation?"

"Six o'clock. I know that's a little early, but it was the only thing available."

"That still gives us plenty of time," he said.

He and Margery beamed at each other while Diana fumed. Hadn't either of them noticed that *she* hadn't agreed to this crazy scheme? She grabbed hold of Margery's arm. "Will you excuse us a moment?" she asked, and dragged her toward the only place she was sure they wouldn't be interrupted.

Once they were safely locked inside the ladies' room, Diana turned to her friend. "What do you think you're doing?" she demanded.

Margery remained calm in the face of Diana's anger. "I'm making sure you have the opportunity to spend the evening in the company of a handsome man to whom you're obviously attracted, who's obviously also attracted to you."

"Jason and I are adults. We don't need you arranging things for us."

Margery had the decency to look chagrined. "Don't think of it as arranging. Think of it as a nudge in the right direction. Though judging from that suit, you were headed there on your own, anyway."

Diana flushed. Maybe she had been thinking of Jason when she put on this suit. Part of her longed for him to see her as an attractive, desirable woman—a potential lover, even though the rest of her was scared of getting in over her head. "Then you'll admit you shouldn't have meddled?" she asked.

"I didn't mean to upset you with my meddling," Margery said. She patted Diana's shoulder. "Think of it this way. You get what you wanted all along—to go out with the man—and don't have to bother making reservations."

"I don't know…" Fear was gaining ground on her bravado. "He thinks my paint colors are too bright." That said everything she needed to know about him.

"Oh, please. As if paint colors really matter." Margery waved off any objections Diana might have made. "That's only surface stuff. Down inside, the two of you are more alike than you think."

"What do you know about it?" Diana asked. "You've only met the man once before."

"But I'm a good listener. I've listened to everything you've told me about him."

"What have I told you?" She honestly couldn't remember. Had she said more than she should have about him?

"He's handsome and sexy. I can see that with my own eyes and, though you might think those things are superficial, you should never underestimate the importance of physical attraction between two people. He's a loving father. He's suffered the tough breakup of his marriage, just as you have. He makes you laugh. And he was worth getting dressed up in that killer suit and heels." Margery grinned. "That's the sexiest outfit you own, so you were obviously hoping for some kind of reaction out of him or you wouldn't have worn it."

Diana blushed once more. "Every other time he's seen me I've been fat and waddling like a hippo in a sack of a maternity outfit," she said. "I wanted to show him there was a real woman underneath all that."

"And did he notice?"

She remembered the heated looks they'd exchanged on the playground. "Yes. He noticed."

"Then take that attention and run with it. Have a nice dinner. See where it leads."

Margery made it sound so easy. Painless. "I don't know," Diana said. "What if—"

"Don't anticipate trouble. Go out and have a good time. For one night. Don't worry about what might happen, just enjoy what *is* happening."

Diana hesitated, then nodded. "All right. One night."
Maybe it would be all she and Jason would have, but
that was all the more reason to make the most of it.

## CHAPTER TWELVE

"WHAT DID YOU and Margery say to each other in the bathroom?" Jason asked as he drove downtown.

"You don't really think I'll tell you, do you?" Diana asked. Buckled in the passenger seat, she felt off balance, unused to being separated from her baby, yet giddy with the prospect of an evening of adult conversation and the company of a handsome, charming man.

"You were talking about me," he said.

"Don't flatter yourself." Though, of course, he was absolutely right. "I was pointing out that I don't need her to play matchmaker for me."

"Is that what she was doing?" His look of exaggerated innocence made her laugh.

"Margery doesn't believe in being subtle," she said.

"So why did you agree to go out with me if you're against her matchmaking?" he asked.

"Maybe I wanted to try this restaurant," she said. "I hear it's very good."

"So you're in it strictly for the dinner."

He did such a poor job of hiding his hurt she had to take pity on him. "I'm in it for the company, too," she said. "It's been a long time since I've shared an evening with a handsome man who wasn't wearing scrubs and telling me to push."

They both began to laugh, and Diana felt as if she could have floated out of the car if her seat belt hadn't been holding her in place.

Jason parked in a garage and they walked down the busy pedestrian mall toward the restaurant. The warm spring weather had brought both tourists and locals out in droves. They crowded the sidewalks in front of stores and restaurants, filled the tables and benches in the center esplanade and piled onto the free trolleys that ran the length of the mall. Conventioneers in business suits, tourists in shorts and T-shirts, groups of teenagers in baggy jeans and homeless men with duffels mingled together in the balmy evening air.

"It's been a while since I've been down here," Jason said, taking her elbow to guide her around a break in the sidewalk. "I'd forgotten what a crazy scene it is."

They passed a horse-drawn carriage awaiting its next passengers. "I love it," she said. "I love the energy of it, and seeing all the different people."

"Hmm." They stopped to wait for the light at a crosswalk. "I find it more draining than energizing," he said. "I've never been one for crowds."

*One more difference between us.* But she pushed the thought away. Tonight she would focus only on what was happening at the moment, without making judgments.

The restaurant was as elegant and cozy as promised. She and Jason breezed past a line of people hoping for a table, and were led to a booth in a secluded corner and presented with menus and a wine list.

"I'll have to skip the wine," she said with a twinge of regret. "I don't think Leah would appreciate it. But you go right ahead if you like."

"That's all right," he said. "Iced tea will be fine."

They studied the menu, but she took the opportunity to study him, as well. Before they'd left his office he'd changed out of the Bugs Bunny tie he'd been wearing, to a more conservative blue-and-silver stripe. When he emerged from the restroom in his suit jacket and the new tie, he'd smelled of spicy cologne, and she suspected he'd shaved, as there was no hint of five-o'clock shadow. She imagined testing the smoothness of his cheeks with her hands and her lips....

"The grilled sea bass sounds good," he said, reminding her she was supposed to be choosing an entrée, not fantasizing about dessert.

"I'll have that," she said, and closed the menu. Anything to keep him from knowing how much he distracted her.

He closed his menu also and for a moment they looked at each other, and the giddy feeling that had overtaken her in the car returned. "You look amazing," he said after a moment. "No one would know you had a baby a month ago."

"Thank you." She owed it all to expensive foundation garments that held everything in and disguised the sags and bags of a forty-year-old body. "And thanks for being such a good sport about this evening," she said.

"I promise I had no idea Margery was going to set us up like this."

"Don't worry about it. I have friends who are always trying to set me up on dates, too, though so far I've managed to dodge them."

"Do you think there's something about some married people that they can't stand to see someone single?" she asked.

"They do say misery loves company." He laughed. "I don't mean that. I know some people are happily married. Maybe they want to share that happiness."

"Or maybe they don't believe someone could truly be happy by themselves," she said.

"Are you?" he asked. "Happy by yourself?"

"Of course I am." She shifted in her chair. "Most of the time."

He nodded, but said nothing more as the waiter arrived to take their order.

"How is your daughter?" she asked after the waiter left.

"She's doing well. Really well. She told me she likes it over there now. She's making friends and settling into a routine." But the sadness of his expression contradicted his words.

"Is something wrong?" Diana asked. "You look upset."

"It's nothing, really." He shrugged. "Candace is pregnant."

"Ouch." Was he upset because the baby wasn't his? Or was it because she'd so clearly moved on with her life? Or was he concerned for his daughter? "What does Kinsey think about this?"

"She's thrilled. It's all she talks about. They're letting her help decorate the nursery, and Candace bought her a life-size doll so they can practice changing its diapers and giving it baths."

The picture of the little girl learning to care for her future brother or sister touched Diana. "That's so sweet. And it sounds as if her mother is doing a good job of making sure she doesn't feel left out."

He nodded, though he didn't seem any happier. Diana knew it hurt him to be left out of so much of his daughter's life. She wished she knew a way to comfort him, to help him focus on the closeness he did share with Kinsey, and not the things that couldn't be changed.

"The custody hearing isn't even scheduled yet," he said, his expression even more glum. "Having to coordinate matters in two countries means everything takes even longer."

"At least you know she's safe and happy while you wait," Diana said. "And you can call her whenever you like."

The waiter arrived with their salads, and he said nothing more on the subject. For the rest of the meal, they talked about single life and caught each other up on the events in their lives. These were the sort of things they had always talked about, but tonight there was a different undercurrent to their conversation, an awareness of each other as man and woman.

Over dessert, Jason asked if she wanted to do something else after dinner. "It's early yet. We could go to a movie or check out a club."

"Maybe some other time. I really need to be getting home." Her breasts were uncomfortably full and, though she had pumped milk for Margery, she didn't want Leah to have too many bottles.

"Of course," he said. "Is this the longest you've been away from Leah?"

"Yes. It feels…odd. I know Margery will take good care of her, but—"

"It's not the same as when you're there to make sure everything is okay. I know the feeling." His smile was wistful.

They took the freeway out of town toward Evergreen. Once away from the city, darkness wrapped around them. In the silence, Diana was more aware of Jason than ever, and aware of her own desire for him.

"I remember driving up this same road hundreds of times as a kid," he said as he exited onto the canyon road that would eventually take them to Evergreen. "My family had a cabin in South Park and we'd come up for weekends in the summer."

"That sounds idyllic," she said. Now it was her turn to be wistful. "My parents had trouble paying rent on one house, much less a second."

"Oh, I'm not talking about a fancy second home— the kind of thing people call a cabin nowadays. This was a one-room log cabin in the National Forest that my grandparents left to my folks."

"Still, it sounds nice. Especially for a kid running around in the woods. Did you go fishing and hiking?"

"Yes." He fell silent, the heavy silence of things left unsaid. "We did all those things before my dad got hurt," he said. "After that, things changed."

"How was your dad hurt?" she asked.

Jason curled his fingers tightly around the steering wheel. "I was twelve," he said. "My dad had recently taken up rock climbing as a hobby. It was something I loved and he thought it would be good for us to do it together. But that day we'd argued about something— I don't even remember what. I was just being a contrary adolescent, I suspect. I ran off in the woods and hid. He decided to go climbing by himself."

"That sounds dangerous," she said.

"It is. It was. He fell and broke his back. A hiker found him and ran for help. He was in a wheelchair for the rest of his life."

"How awful!"

Jason cleared his throat. "I got back to the cabin just as the sheriff showed up to give us the news. I was sure it was my fault for not going with him."

"But you were just a child. He never should have gone by himself."

"I know that now, but when you're twelve years old and the father you always looked up to is suddenly helpless…" He took a deep breath. "Things really changed for my family after that. We still came to the cabin from time to time, but it wasn't the same. We had it modified for Dad's wheelchair, but my mom pretty much fell apart after the accident. She'd always relied on Dad to look after her. Even when he wasn't capable of doing things for her anymore, she refused to pump her own gas or mow the lawn. So I ended up doing those things."

Diana had an image of Jason at twelve, burdened by guilt, trying to be the man of the house. Was that what drove his need to always be in charge now? "That's a lot for a boy to take on," she said.

"My dad died when I was in college, and my sisters and I persuaded Mom to move into a town home community in Fort Collins. Six months later, she married a neighbor and they moved to Sun City."

"I'm sorry you had to lose your dad so young."

"Thanks. So, that's my story. What's yours? Are both your parents still around?"

"In a manner of speaking. They're living in a commune in New Mexico. They've always been sort of free spirits. I was an only child and got used to looking after myself from a pretty young age." By the time she was a teenager she'd sometimes felt as if she was the parent and her mom and dad were the children.

"I think my dad's accident is what led me to want to be a teacher," Jason said. "I wanted to help children. To be someone they could depend on."

*Because there wasn't anyone for you to depend on as a child,* she thought. She knew what that was like, the fear and insecurity of believing everything depended on you, even though you were only ten or twelve or fifteen—too young to bear such a burden. That had to be why Richard—mature, financially stable, take-charge Richard—had held such a strong attraction for her.

She reached across the seat and clasped Jason's hand in her own. He squeezed it gently, a silent message of thanks and understanding. They said nothing, but continued to hold hands the rest of the way back to the school.

He parked near her car and came around to open the door for her. Though the lot was unlit, the almost-full moon and hundreds of stars glittering overhead bathed them in a soft glow. "I can't get over how much brighter the stars are here than in the city," she said, looking up.

"Not as bright as you look to me."

The husky note of his voice sent a tremor through her. Their gazes met and he took her into his arms. His lips claimed hers with an assuredness that blotted out any lingering doubts she might have had about his feelings for her. All that mattered in this moment was the feel of his mouth against hers, of his tongue teasing her lips and his hand caressing her side. She stood on tiptoe, her body arched to his, pressed against the muscular wall of his chest and the hard evidence of his desire. He dragged one hand up to cup her breast, and she moaned softly as a thrill of arousal coursed through her.

But beneath the outright lust and need ran other feelings, emotions she hadn't allowed herself to experience since the day Richard had abandoned her and her child: the heady sensations of being supported and cared for and protected completely. Such surrender felt as dangerous and forbidden as an illegal drug, and every bit as thrilling and intoxicating.

Breathless, her heart pounding, she pulled away from him slightly. "I really have to go," she said, but made no move to release her hold on him.

"Yeah." He rested his forehead against hers, his breathing ragged. "I guess I got a little carried away there. I'm s—"

She covered his mouth with her fingers. "Don't apologize. I certainly won't."

"Then *I* won't." He sucked the tips of her fingers into his mouth and her knees buckled. If he could make her feel this way merely by kissing her fingers…

Some last reserve of willpower enabled her to stand on her own feet and pull away from him once more. "I really do have to go," she said.

He nodded. "I know." He kept his arm around her all the way to her car, and gave her one last knee-weakening kiss before he finally surrendered her. "Be careful," he said.

She nodded. "Good night."

She had to try three times before her shaking hand fit the key in the lock. She pulled out of the lot, then glanced in her rearview mirror. Jason was still standing there, watching her drive away, a solitary figure silhouetted in the moonlight.

THE NEXT DAY, all Jason wanted was to call Diana, but circumstances conspired against him finding the privacy to do so. He went through the motions of going to work and attending meetings, but his mind was always on her.

He wanted to talk to her, to reassure himself that what had happened in the parking lot had not been a fevered dream, but reality. Something had broken in him during their drive up the canyon, some last reserve that had kept his desire for her safely walled off from what he knew to be right and practical. Remembering those harrowing, guilt-ridden days immediately after his father's accident had reminded him how quickly everything could change, and how important it was to enjoy what he had right now.

What he'd had in the parking lot was Diana in his arms. Not Diana the mother of a newborn or Diana the artist, but Diana the woman. And he hadn't been a superintendent or a father or a man with responsibilities to anyone but himself. He wanted her; she wanted him. It was exhilarating to have life reduced to a formula as simple as that.

Less than twenty-four hours had passed since that moment, and already it had faded to fuzzy memory. Could it really have been as intense as it seemed? Did it mean more than a kiss in a parking lot? And what the hell did it mean for their future?

He might have called and asked her all these questions, but it was a conversation that required privacy, one thing he didn't have right now. As soon as he finished work for the day, Graham had arrived to set up the webcam so that he and Kinsey could see each other whenever they talked on the phone.

"You sent her all the equipment I got for you?" Graham asked as he unpacked a box of cables, CDs, instruction booklets and the small camera that would mount on Jason's computer monitor.

"Yes. She said Victor promised to hook everything up by this weekend."

"What's this French guy like, anyway?"

"He's an actor."

"Is he any good?"

"I don't know. I don't care."

"Has he been in anything I might have seen?"

"Not unless you've been taking trips to Paris. He's in the theater, not the movies."

"Oh." Graham crawled behind the desk and began fiddling with various cables and cords. "Is he good-looking?"

"How the hell should I know?"

"I'll bet he is. Actors have to be, don't they? Besides, Candace is a looker, so it stands to reason she wouldn't hook up with some ugly mutt—even if she was married to you."

"Just hook up the camera."

Graham emerged from behind the desk and fed a CD into the computer. "Speaking of good-looking women, wasn't that Diana Shelton I saw you with at the school yesterday afternoon?"

"Yes." Jason kept his expression indifferent. He picked up a pencil and began turning it over and over in his hand. "She came by to check on the progress of the construction."

Graham let out a low whistle. "I don't think I realized before what a terrific body was hiding beneath those maternity clothes."

Jason tightened his grip on the pencil. It was either that or give in to the urge to punch Graham. He didn't want to think too much about whether his annoyance at his friend stemmed from Graham's incessant teasing or the knowledge that he'd been ogling Diana.

"Have you asked her out yet?"

The pencil snapped.

Graham regarded him with one eyebrow raised. "Is that a yes or a no?"

"We had dinner last night."

"And?"

"And what? It was a very pleasant evening."

"Pleasant?" Graham shook his head. "I was expecting better of you than that." He turned his attention back to the computer and typed something in. "Did you at least kiss her?"

"What, are we back in high school now? I have to give you a full report?"

"You don't have to tell me anything. But I think you should kiss her. It might improve your disposition."

All kissing Diana had done was confuse his feelings even further. "Is the camera hooked up yet?"

"The camera is hooked up." Graham pushed the chair back from the desk. "Just click this icon here and log in and you're ready to go." He stood and clapped Jason on the back. "I've got to get out of here. I promised Denise I'd take our youngest to a birthday party while she's pulling soccer duty with the older girls."

"Thanks, Graham. I really appreciate it."

"Anytime. And if you need any tips for getting back into the swing of things with Diana, I'm your man."

"Right. You haven't dated in fifteen years."

"You're wrong. Denise and I go out every Thursday night. That kind of romancing is even more important after you've said 'I do.'" He grinned. "And I must be doing something right—I've got six kids."

"No comment. Thanks again for your help with the webcam."

"Let me know if you have any problems."

He had problems, all right, but none Graham could fix. When his friend was gone, Jason returned to the computer and experimented with the camera. A check of the clock showed it was 7:00 p.m. in Paris—not too late to call. He could nag Victor about hooking up the webcam on his end.

The man himself answered the phone, his voice smooth and heavily accented. *"Allô?"*

"This is Jason Benton. I'd like to speak to my daughter."

"Oh, hello, Jason." He spoke flawless English. "Kinsey will be pleased to hear from you. I will get her."

Seconds later, Kinsey's excited voice filled his ear. "Daddy! I'm so glad you called. Do you have your camera on your computer?"

"I do. I was calling to see if you had yours."

"We do! Victor put it in this morning. Wait, and I'll turn

it on." She said something in French, and Victor replied, also in French. Jason cursed his ignorance of the language.

"Look at your computer, Daddy. Are you there?"

"I'm here." He glanced at the screen and there was Kinsey, grinning and waving at him. His heart skipped a beat at the sight of her, and he swallowed a knot of tears. "You look beautiful, sweet pea," he said. He couldn't believe how much she'd changed since his last visit. She appeared taller, her face less full, though maybe that was the new hairstyle. Gone were the pigtails he remembered, replaced by a chic, shorter cut. Even her clothes—a boat neck T-shirt and dark shorts— looked more French.

"I can see you, too," Kinsey said. "I remember that shirt. You used to wear it all the time on Saturdays."

He glanced down at the Colorado Rockies T-shirt. It was an old favorite, faded but comfortable.

"How do you like my new haircut?" Kinsey preened for the camera.

"It's very nice," he said. "Very grown-up." He didn't want his daughter to grow up this quickly—not without him there to see.

"A friend of Victor's cut it for me. Mademoiselle Gigot from the theater."

The camera wobbled and Victor appeared behind her, as handsome and suave as Jason remembered. "You mustn't bounce so, *ma chère,*" he said. "It makes the camera move."

"I'll try to be still." Kinsey held her wrist up to the

camera. "See my new bracelet?" she said. "Victor got it for me this morning at the market. And we bought a pretty mobile for the baby's room. I picked it out."

"That's great." Jason struggled to get the words out, and to keep the smile on his face. The thought of Kinsey spending her days with another man, receiving presents from him, anticipating the arrival of a baby brother or sister that Jason had no part of, tore at him.

Kinsey chattered on about her friends at school, a movie she had seen and the new dress she had to wear to Candace's gallery opening the following week. "It's a silky blue fabric with little glass beads. When I put it on, I'll call you so you can see."

"I'd like that," he said. "You'll be beautiful. You're already beautiful."

"Thank you, Daddy." Her voice grew wistful. "I wish you were here to go with us. You could see my dress and you could see Mama's paintings and meet the baby. Of course, you couldn't actually meet him, because he's still inside Mama, but you could see how he's growing inside her."

"I'm sorry I can't be there," he said. "But it won't be long before it will be time for you to visit me."

"That's right! I can't wait to see you."

Victor said something in French. Kinsey looked over her shoulder toward him, then turned back to the camera. "I have to go now. We're having dinner with some friends. Goodbye, Daddy. I love you." She blew kisses to the camera, then dissolved into giggles.

"I love you, too," he said.

Then the screen went black. He stared at it, seeing only his own dim reflection in the glare. Maybe the camera had been a bad idea. He'd looked forward to seeing Kinsey, thinking it would make him feel closer to her. Instead, the pictures emphasized the distance between them. She was changing so fast, with new clothes, new friends and even a new haircut. While he was stuck here, looking the same to her as before she'd moved away. He was her father, whom she loved and talked to on the phone once a week. But Victor was the man who helped her with her homework and bought her presents and was there every day.

Jason pressed the heel of his hand to the bridge of his nose, fighting tears. He had to get out of the house. Find something to distract himself so that he could remain strong and in control.

## CHAPTER THIRTEEN

DIANA STARED at the arrangement of roses, lilies and delphiniums a florist had just delivered. She reread the card again, unable to believe her eyes.

I miss you. Give me a second chance. We belong together.
Love, Richard.

The plaintiveness of his words touched her, but only as she might feel pity for any acquaintance going through rough emotional waters. She remembered the sadness in his eyes when he'd pleaded with her at the baby shower—and his attempt to persuade her with the promise of a Roman vacation that proved he was acting only in his own self-interest. She could never go back to being Mrs. Richard Shelton, her life revolving around her husband and what he wanted to do.

Yes, she was lonely. And after the instability and uncertainty of her childhood, it had been comforting to be taken care of. But for Richard, caretaking too often meant smothering her. He was a man used to making all the decisions, and she didn't want to invest the energy into trying to change him.

The ringing doorbell interrupted her thoughts. She cautiously checked the peephole and was startled to see Jason.

She opened the door. "Jason." He looked terrible, his face haggard, hair mussed, the shadow of a beard along his jaw.

"Can I come in?" he asked.

"Of course." She stood aside to let him pass. "Has something happened? Is something wrong?"

"No. Yes. I don't know. I just… I needed to talk to someone."

"Come into the kitchen. Have you eaten?"

"I had a burger a while ago. I'm not hungry." He followed her into the brightly lit room.

"Let me make you some tea." One thing Diana's mother had passed on to her was a love of herbal teas and a belief in their calming powers. She set the water to boil and took two cups and tea bags from the cabinet. Jason sat slumped at the table, silent.

Neither said anything until the tea was poured and she sat across from him. "What's wrong?" she asked.

"My friend Graham installed a webcam on my computer, so that Kinsey and I could see each other when we talked."

"That's a great idea." But he didn't look happy about it. "Isn't it?"

"I thought it would be. But I hadn't anticipated how hard it would be to see her." He slumped further in the chair, and cradled the teacup in both hands. "She's grown so much in these past few weeks. She has a new haircut and…" His voice died and he stared morosely into the cup.

She reached across and clasped his hand. "I'm sorry. I'm sure it is hard. But I'm also sure she liked seeing you."

He nodded. "She did. She's obviously much happier now than she was when she and her mother first moved to Paris."

"That's good."

"Yes…" He sipped his tea. "I'm worried she won't be happy here now. Evergreen, Colorado, is very different from Paris, France."

"Are you considering dropping your custody suit?"

"No. I don't know. I don't know what to do. I don't want to talk about it right now." His gaze met hers. "I just…I didn't want to be alone."

"Then I'm glad you came here."

They sipped their tea in silence, but the air was charged with awareness now. She remembered the kiss they'd shared last night—a kiss that could so easily have led to more.

"How are you doing?" he asked, sitting up straighter and making an obvious attempt to pull himself together. "How is the baby?"

"We're both fine. I just put her down for a nap. Would you like to see her?"

"Not right now." He pushed aside his cup and looked directly at Diana. "I've been divorced over a year, separated a year before that, and in that time I've avoided getting involved with another woman. I told myself I was doing it for Kinsey. I didn't want her to have to adjust to another change in her life, and I wanted to keep myself free to focus on her. But those were all excuses. The reason I didn't date—the reason I didn't let myself get close to anyone—was because I was afraid of making another mistake. I didn't want to go through that…that pain again."

"I know," she whispered, touched by his candor. She cleared her throat. "I know I made the right decision to leave Richard. We weren't right for each other and I was suffocating in our marriage. But knowing that doesn't make the pain of his rejection any easier to take. I think when a person has been hurt like that, it's only natural they wouldn't want to go through it again."

"Then what do you do?" he asked. "Live your whole life behind a protective wall?"

"No. You have to find a way to reach out. To climb over that wall." She squeezed his hand.

He stood and pulled her to him, the movement sudden and surprising and yet inevitable. They kissed, a long, melting embrace that left her breathless and wanting more. "I'm ready to climb over that wall if you're ready to climb with me," he said.

"Yes," she said. "I think it's about time."

Holding tightly to his hand, she led the way toward her bedroom, pausing to glance in at the baby. Leah slept soundly, tiny fists curled on either side of her face.

"We'll be able to hear her if she needs us," Jason said.

She nodded and continued down the hall to her bedroom. As usual, the bed wasn't made, and her clothes were scattered about, but she didn't care. If he wanted her, he had to take all of her, messy habits and everything.

She turned to him and wrapped her arms around him.

"Are you nervous?" he asked.

"No." The answer surprised her; she had expected when this moment came she'd be shaking in her shoes. But she felt only a steadying calm, and the happiness of anticipation. "We're alone," she said. "And neither one of us has to be afraid."


JASON FUMBLED WITH the buttons of her blouse, feeling as clumsy as a boy—in a hurry, yet wanting to savor the moment. She reached up to help him, then pushed her hands beneath his shirt, sliding her palms across his stomach and up his chest, sending heat coursing through him.

He grasped the hem and stripped off the shirt, then helped her out of her blouse and jeans, the nursing bra and bikini underwear. When they were both naked, he stepped back to admire her full round breasts and hourglass curve of waist and hips.

She ducked her head and crawled into bed, pulling the covers to her chin. He climbed in beside her, and slowly peeled the blankets away. "I want to look at you," he said. He smoothed one hand along her rib cage, then traced the web of stretch marks across her stomach.

"Don't," she protested, covering his hand with her own.

"They're beautiful," he said, and bent to kiss the fine, pale lines. They were the marks of a woman who had given birth, who had paid the price with her body to bring a new life into the world.

She trembled beneath him. He was shaking, too, no longer with nervousness, but with anticipation. It had been so long he hoped he didn't disgrace himself. He forced himself to take deep breaths, to slow both his thoughts and his movements.

To take time to enjoy this moment with this very special woman.

Her hands moved lightly across his skin, tracing the contours of his body, caressing his back and arms and buttocks. "You feel so good," she murmured, arching against him.

He stilled.

"What is it?" she asked. "Is something wrong?"

Sighing, he drew back and met her gaze. "We should probably use a condom," he said. "I know the chance is slight, but you could still get pregnant."

"You're right."

His spirits sank. "It's not something I carry around with me. I don't suppose…?" But what would a new mother be doing with condoms?

Her mouth quirked in a half smile. "Promise not to laugh?"

"I promise."

"I think I have one. In the medicine cabinet." She

slipped from the bed and hurried into the bathroom. He propped his head on his elbow, enjoying the sight of her moving through the semidarkness.

She reappeared after a minute or so, holding a square foil packet aloft like a trophy.

"What are you doing with *one* condom?" he asked as she crawled into bed beside him and handed it to him.

"Margery gave it to me. Part of a shower gift—a bag full of all kinds of stuff I was supposed to use after the baby was born. Bubble bath and chocolates, a new nightgown, lotion—all kinds of things. Including this."

"I like the way Margery thinks." He ripped open the packet.

"She did it to embarrass me in front of all the shower guests," Diana said. "At the time I wanted to strangle her, but now I'm grateful for her twisted sense of humor."

"Me, too." He rolled on the condom, aware of her watching him. Her breathing quickened and she let out a soft moan that was almost his undoing.

When he glanced at her, she put her arms around his neck and pulled him down beside her, kissing him with renewed urgency.

He caressed her hips, then moved his hand between her legs. "I don't want to hurt you," he whispered, stroking her gently.

Her breath caught. "You won't. The doctor says I'm completely healed. We'll just take it slow and easy."

Taking it slow wasn't easy for him, not now that he was here with her. But he forced himself to put aside his own need, to focus on her. He continued to stroke and caress her, feeling her body tense beneath him, her breath coming in little gasps of pleasure that fueled his own desire. He slid two fingers into her while continuing to stroke her with his thumb, and felt her tighten around him. Her eyes half closed and her lips curved in a look of pure bliss. A rosy flush spread across her cheeks. He bent and traced the curve of her breast with his tongue, and felt her shudder.

"Jason!" she gasped, and clutched at him.

Quickly, he knelt between her legs and entered her, forcing himself to move carefully, watching her face for any sign of discomfort on her part. Smiling, she grasped his hips and pulled him toward her. "Don't be afraid of hurting me," she said. "This feels wonderful." She rocked against him, as if to emphasize her words, and clamped her legs around him.

He closed his eyes and surrendered to his own growing need. Encouraged by her stroking hands and the rocking of her hips, he raced toward a shuddering climax that left him joyous and spent.

They lay together for a minute or more, unmoving, hearts pounding in unison. Gradually, sense returned, and he moved off of her. "Sorry, didn't mean to crush you," he said.

"It's all right."

He wrapped the spent condom in tissue and discarded it in the trash can beside the bed. They held each other close for many minutes, not speaking, not needing to speak, until the baby began to cry.

"She's probably hungry," Diana said, sitting and reaching for her robe.

He lay back and listened as she padded down the hall. The soft murmur of her voice broadcast over the baby monitor, along with Leah's answering cries. He smiled, reveling in the joy of such sweet domestic sounds.

She returned with the child in her arms and settled into bed beside him once more. He watched as she folded back her robe and put the baby to her breast. "That brings back memories," he said. How many times had he watched Candace nurse Kinsey this way?

"It's something I don't want to ever forget." She caressed the baby's head and her eyes met his. "I won't forget this evening, either."

"No." He smiled and idly stroked her thigh. He couldn't remember when he'd last felt so at peace.

He dozed, and was awakened by the doorbell chime, loud and discordant in the bedroom silence.

"Who in the world?" Diana sat up straight and stared toward the living room. The bell sounded again, and Leah began to cry.

"Were you expecting someone?" Jason asked.

"No." She laid the baby in the middle of the bed and reached for her clothes.

"Don't answer it," he said. "Whoever it is will think you're not home, and leave."

She hesitated. "Your car's out front."

"How many of your friends know that's my car?"

The bell sounded again, followed by pounding on

the door. "Diana!" a man's voice demanded. "Open up. It's me."

Jason plucked his jeans from the floor and pulled them on. "Who is it?" he asked.

Diana's face flushed, and her eyes sparked with anger. "It's Richard," she said. "What is *he* doing here?"

DIANA FUMBLED with the buttons of her blouse as Richard continued to pound on the door, and Leah wailed louder. No use pretending she wasn't here. He'd have heard the baby by now.

She picked up her daughter and cradled her close. Jason finished zipping his jeans and bent to retrieve his shirt. Renewed desire fluttered through her at the memory of the feel of his muscular back beneath her hands. She quickly looked away. "I'd better answer that," she said.

Richard's hand was raised in the act of knocking when she jerked open the door. He lowered it, only a slight redness in his face betraying any agitation. His voice when he spoke was calm. "Diana, what took you so long?" he asked.

"What are you doing here?" she asked.

"I came to see you." He moved past her, into the living room. "I see you got the flowers I sent."

"Yes, but I really—"

"Did you get a new car? What's it doing in the driveway? You should park it in the garage."

"That's my car."

Diana stifled a groan as Jason walked into the room. Fully dressed, hair neatly combed, he didn't look like a man who'd spent the last hour in bed with a woman, but Richard was smart enough to realize there were few other things a man would be doing in the back of her house at this hour of night.

"Who are you?" Richard asked, clearly startled.

"Jason Benton." He didn't offer his hand. The two men squared off like two bull elk about to do battle over a cow—*her*.

"Richard, what are you doing here?" she demanded again.

"I came to discuss when you and the baby would be moving home," he said.

"Moving home?" Jason's voice was loud, perhaps louder than he'd intended.

Diana shifted the baby to her other shoulder. "I'm not moving anywhere," she said. "I'm staying right here."

Richard looked pained, the way he appeared in a restaurant when the waiter got his order wrong and he had to send it back. "Now that I've made it clear I want you back, why would you want to stay here?" he asked.

Jason stared, apparently keen to hear her answer also. "We're divorced, Richard," she said. "I'm not your wife anymore. Your home is not my home."

"I said I'm sorry. What more do you want? We can make a fresh start. We can even have more children, if you like."

Clearly, she was losing her mind. This couldn't be Richard saying these things. Yet behind his words was the same attitude that was his trademark: the assumption that she would do whatever he wanted.

Not this time. "No," she said. "I'm not moving back. We can't start again. Our marriage is over."

He frowned, and turned his attention to Jason. "Is it because of him?" He looked the younger man up and down. Diana knew when understanding dawned. Richard's face looked pinched and older. "Is that why his car's in your driveway? Because you've been sleeping with him?"

"I don't think that's any of your business," Jason said.

"What the mother of my child does *is* my business," Richard barked.

Since when had Richard been so concerned about his daughter? He hadn't even asked about her this evening. "Richard, you need to go," Diana said.

"You heard the lady," Jason said, stepping forward as if to escort Richard out.

"You should go, too, Jason." She turned to him. "I'd really like to be alone now."

The two men glared at each other. Neither of them wanted to be the first to leave. "Now, Diana, don't be that way." Richard offered a placating smile. "You and I have a lot to talk about. If we could just sit down—"

"No, Richard. I don't have anything to say to you."

"Are you sure you don't want me to stay?" Jason asked.

"No." Just because she'd had sex with him didn't mean she was ready for him to move in. "It's getting late and I need to look after Leah."

"I can help you," Jason said.

"No."

He was smart enough to give in. "After you," he said to Richard.

Richard opened his mouth as if to argue further, but Diana cut him off. "Good night," she said firmly, and left the room.

In the shelter of the darkened hallway, she turned to watch them. The two men glared at each other, fists clenched at their sides. Diana didn't think either of them would stoop to throwing punches, but she wished she had the phone close by, just in case.

After a long minute of tense silence, Richard gathered himself and abruptly left, shutting the door softly behind him. Jason lingered a moment, then glanced toward the hallway. Diana retreated farther into the darkness. "Diana?" he said.

"Good night, Jason."

Another long moment of silence. "Good night."

She waited until she heard his car start, then walked to the door and locked it. Forehead pressed to the wood, she let out a long sigh.

This was the problem with letting a man back into her life—all the expectations and determination to make her do what *he* wanted her to do, rarely considering what *she* wanted. Was not being alone really worth all the hassle?

# CHAPTER FOURTEEN

SHE'D KICKED HIM OUT. Jason spent the rest of the weekend trying to wrap his mind around this reality. He and Diana had been enjoying a blissful time together, then her ex-husband had shown up and everything had changed.

She'd said she didn't want to get back together with Richard, but was that true? She must have some attachment to him, considering they'd stayed together eighteen years. He wasn't bad looking, and he obviously had money—the Jag he'd driven away in wasn't the kind of car school superintendents could afford, that was for sure.

Jason shook his head. No. He'd seen the look in Diana's eyes when Richard had made his offer. She had no intention of ever going back to him.

So why had her expression been disturbingly similar when she'd looked at Jason?

"Hey, where were you Saturday night?" Graham stopped by Jason's office Monday morning before class. "Denise and I called to invite you over for barbecue, but you weren't answering your phone."

"I was out." He shuffled papers on his desk, avoiding Graham's eyes.

"Out? Where? With whom?"

"None of your business."

"Hey, no need to bite my head off. I was merely curious. As a friend."

Graham's injured tone stung. Jason shoved the paperwork aside. Maybe confiding in someone would help him gain perspective. "Come in and close the door," he said.

Graham did as requested. "So what's the big secret?" he asked.

"I was with Diana," Jason said.

"Ohhhhh." Graham grinned. "Congratulations. I'm proud of you for finally asking her out."

He didn't bother explaining that he hadn't asked her out; he'd shown up on her doorstep, desperate and lonely, and she'd invited him into her home—and her bed. "Yeah, it was great. Until her ex showed up."

"Her ex showed up? The baby's father?"

Jason nodded. "They had words and she kicked him out—then asked me to leave, too."

"Ouch."

"Yeah. I tried to change her mind, but she wasn't having any of it."

"I imagine her ex spoiled the mood. Maybe she was tired. Have you talked to her since? Taken a reading on the situation?"

"I've tried, but she isn't answering her phone and she hasn't returned my messages."

"Maybe she had to go out of town?"

The idea lightened his mood. "I hadn't thought of that. She didn't mention anything about that Saturday."

"Maybe it came up suddenly."

"Maybe so." Though that still didn't explain why she hadn't responded to the voice mails he'd left on her cell phone. "This is what drives me nuts about women," he said. "They're so unpredictable."

"They probably say the same thing about us," Graham said. "And let's face it, if there wasn't some mystery, would we be as intrigued?"

"Maybe not," Jason said grudgingly. It wouldn't be so bad if all the surprises about women were good ones. It was the bad ones—like being left or being asked to leave—that hurt.

"Did you talk to Kinsey yet? Did the camera setup work?"

"It worked great. Thanks."

"How's she doing?"

"Good. Better than I expected. She has a new haircut. Very French. And she's excited about Candace's new baby. Candace has a showing at a gallery next week. And I gather Victor is in a new play."

"Sounds as if things are going well for all of them."

"Yeah." Jason drummed his fingers on the desk. "I've been thinking. Kinsey isn't living the life I wanted for her, but she seems happy, and I can see she's well taken care of. Candace is…flighty sometimes. But she's a good mom."

"Yes, she is," Graham said. "And I always thought her creativity and flightiness balanced out your more regimented approach."

So even Graham thought Jason was a control freak.

"I'm thinking of dropping the custody suit," he said. "Candace and I screwed up our marriage. I don't want to compound the problem by uprooting Kinsey all over again, or by making her the rope in a game of tug-of-war."

"I think that's a wise decision," Graham said. "Not an easy one, but wise."

"She's coming here for the summer." Jason held on to this truth like a shipwrecked sailor to a raft. "And when she's older, she always has the option of moving here."

"And you can keep video conferencing with her and flying over for visits when you can," Graham said. "It's not the old, traditional family structure, but children are more flexible than we give them credit for. You'll make it work."

"Yeah, we will." But shouldn't doing the right thing feel better than this?

"I'd better get to class." Graham stood. "Let me know what happens with Diana."

"Yeah." When his friend had left, Jason stared at the phone on his desk. Should he try to call Diana one more time?

He shook his head and tried to focus on a report he needed to compile, but when his phone rang, he answered it before the second note had died away. "Hello?"

"Hi, Jason." Diana's voice, musical and soft, made his heart race. "I'm sorry I didn't return your calls earlier," she said. "I spent the weekend thinking."

*About us?* He wanted to ask, but settled for a noncommittal, "Yes?"

"It was wonderful being with you Saturday night," she said. "Magical."

"Yes, it was." Magical was the perfect way to describe their lovemaking, and the peaceful companionship afterward.

"Yes, but I think we'd better leave it at that and not try to take a relationship any further," she said. "I'm not ready for a full-time commitment to anyone. Richard's visit made me see that."

"I'm not Richard," he protested.

"No. But you have a lot in common. It's probably why I was so attracted to you." Her voice softened. "Be honest, Jason. I'd drive you crazy. I'm disorganized and spontaneous and not punctual—all the things you hate."

"I'm not as inflexible as you seem to think."

"You're a muted-colors kind of person. I'm bright purple and yellow. If we can't even agree on colors for a playscape, how would we ever last as a couple?"

Everything she said was logical and sensible, the kind of argument he might have made himself. Yet he wanted to shout that she was wrong. All those differences weren't important if they loved each other.

Yet they'd made a difference, in the end, with him and Candace. They had mattered to Diana when she'd left Richard. How could she and Jason pretend their opposite traits weren't important when experience had taught them otherwise? "Maybe you're right," he said reluctantly. "Breaking it off now is probably the sensible thing to do." For once, he didn't want to be sensible.

"This doesn't mean we can't still be friends," she said.

"Of course not." Were there ever more damning words to end a romance?

"We'll stay in touch. I probably won't see you for a while. Construction on the playscape is going well, so there's no reason for me to visit the school."

"Right. Well, see you around, I guess."

"Take care."

So that was it. An exchange of lame goodbyes and meaningless promises to remain in contact. The kind of promises people never really kept. She was busy with her baby and business, and he had work to keep him occupied. Kinsey would arrive from Paris in a few weeks and he'd soon forget all about Diana.

Except he knew he wouldn't. Diana was someone he'd remember forever, always with a touch of regret for what might have been.

"ARE YOU OUT OF YOUR freaking mind?"

Margery's reaction to the news that Diana had slept with, then broken up with Jason was not what Diana had hoped for.

"That man is perfect for you," Margery continued. "He's crazy about you, and about Leah."

The two friends were walking in the park with Leah in her stroller. "He's all wrong for me," Diana said, walking faster to keep up with Margery's angry strides. "He's a control freak like Richard. Another man who'll try to fit me into a mold of his making."

"Being organized and logical and a little conservative does not automatically translate to control freak," Margery said. "And you're wrong about him being like Richard. Jason loves children. You told me so yourself."

"Yes, he loves children. And he's a good father. That doesn't mean he'd be a good husband. He already has one failed marriage behind him."

"That's rich, coming from someone who's divorced herself."

Diana winced. "You know what I mean. His first wife was an artist. A creative type like me."

"All that proves is that something in him is attracted to artistic women. Just as you're apparently attracted to responsible men."

"Right. Responsible men like Richard. Who hasn't stopped calling since Saturday night. I had to quit answering the phone." Just as well, since it had helped her avoid talking to Jason before she'd had time to think.

"You're going to have to get tough," Margery said. "Make it clear you're never coming back to him."

"I have made it clear. I've been tough."

"You are many things, dear, but tough is not one of them."

"He *is* Leah's father. I can't refuse to talk to him at all."

"Why not? If he's so interested in his daughter, he can go to court and ask for visitation. Has he even asked about her?"

Diana shook her head. "You're right. I need to tell

him to get lost. I'd hoped he'd get the message without me having to lose my temper with him."

"If you were involved with someone else, he'd get the message."

"I am *not* going to start a relationship with someone just so Richard will leave me alone."

Margery shrugged. "You obviously need some kind of incentive. Thought I'd give that one a try."

"Why are you being so contrary?" Diana griped.

"Because you haven't given me one good reason why you dumped Jason. Was he lousy in bed?"

"No!" Diana's cheeks grew hot. "And I didn't dump him. We agreed we'd still be friends."

They passed a playscape featuring an underwater theme, with sea horse-shaped swings and a slide down a whale's tail. Diana hadn't designed it, but it was one of her favorites.

"What are you going to do about finishing the playscape at Jason's school?" Margery asked.

"I don't have to do anything. The contractor is taking care of it."

"You'll need to stop by and check on it, won't you?"

"Not necessarily."

"I think you should. If only to show your *friend,* Jason, that you're on top of things."

"Margery, let it go."

"No, I won't. You want to have your cake and eat it, too. You want the pleasure of Jason's company without the pressures of commitment. Do you really think you can be friends with a man you're in love with?"

Diana's stomach clenched. "I never said I was in love with him."

"You didn't have to. All anyone had to do was see the two of you together."

"What did you see?" Diana slowed and turned to her friend. "Why would you think we're in love when we're not even sure ourselves?"

"It was all there in your eyes," Margery said. "The way you looked at each other as if the rest of the world didn't exist. The way you turned toward each other. The way you smiled. Like two people who were meant to be together."

"You saw all that?" Diana asked.

Margery nodded. "I did. Which is why I'm so upset you'd throw all that away because you're afraid."

"I am not afraid." She gripped the handle of the stroller and started forward again.

"Then what is going on inside that head of yours? Here you have a chance to be with a good-looking, stable man who's crazy about you and your daughter. You're crazy about him, too. So what if the two of you aren't exactly alike? Does the fact that he folds his clothes before getting into bed or washes his car every week really matter enough to throw away the chance for love and happiness?"

"How did you know he folds his clothes?"

Margery smiled. "I know the type. Before I married my absentminded professor, I dated a few other men, including an engineer who not only folded his clothes, but perfectly aligned his shoes on the edge of the rug."

"But you didn't marry him."

"No. But I didn't *love* him."

And Diana loved Jason. Margery was right about that. But she was wrong about everything else. Diana could be friends with Jason. And she could be tough. Tough and independent and a woman who didn't need anyone else to make her happy.

DIANA BEGAN WORKING full-time again, as much to distract herself from brooding about Jason as to get her business back up to full speed. Leah traveled with her wherever she went, and Diana became an expert at juggling car seat, diaper bag and briefcase.

Two weeks after she'd asked Jason to leave her home, she received an excited telephone call from Steve. "We're getting a baby!" he said. "We just got the call. Not an infant—a three-year-old. His name is Micah and he has black hair and he's adorable."

"I can't believe it happened so fast," Diana said. She had known couples who waited years for a child.

"I know. We were in the right place at the right time. We're picking him up this afternoon. I'm so excited I can't breathe."

"Congratulations," Diana said. "You and Eric will be wonderful fathers."

"I hope so. I have to go now. I have a long list of people to call, but I wanted you to be the first to know."

That weekend, the young men held a barbecue to introduce friends and family. A thin boy with beautiful brown eyes and black curls, Micah clung to Eric and Steve, smiling shyly at the guests who made a fuss over him.

"Is he settling in all right?" Diana asked when Eric had taken Micah to the kitchen to help him with the cooking.

"He's had some nightmares, and one meltdown, but we expected it," Steve said with a calm acceptance that impressed Diana. "He was taken from an abusive situation and is developmentally delayed, but he's already in therapy and his caseworker thinks there's an excellent chance he'll grow up to be perfectly normal—or as normal as any of us are."

"That's wonderful," Diana said.

"I hope he's all right," Claire said. She and Derek had arrived on time for once, with a gift of a toy truck that had made Micah's eyes light up. "It's going to be hard enough explaining you two to my kid without having to deal with a nutty cousin, too."

"Claire!" Diana scolded.

"Steve knows I don't mean anything by it," Claire said. "Anyway, didn't you pay attention to what I said. *My kid.*" A grin split her face.

"Does this mean you're finally pregnant?" Steve asked.

"Yes!" She wrapped both arms around her stomach. "Eight weeks."

"Congratulations," Diana said. She wanted to be happy for her stepdaughter, though considering Claire hadn't even been interested enough to take care of a dog, Diana had her doubts. She knew what it was like to grow up with self-centered parents.

But unlike Diana's solitary childhood, this baby would have family around to make sure it was loved and looked after. Steve and Diana and many others would be looking out for it.

"I hope the kid takes after its father, not its mother," Steve said. "It's going to be hard enough to explain *you* to *my* kid."

Claire stuck her tongue out at her brother while the others laughed.

"Is Dad still giving you a hard time?" Steve asked Diana.

"No, he isn't."

"How did you finally convince him you weren't interested in getting back together?" he asked.

"He wasn't taking a straightforward no for an answer, so I told him I wanted more children. Many more. That I thought I'd like to try for twins or triplets. With all those babies, I wouldn't be able to travel, or play hostess at parties for his fellow academics and, of course, that would probably ruin my looks. He couldn't run away fast enough." She laughed. The expression on Richard's face when she'd delivered this news had been priceless.

"But…I thought we could go back to the way things were," he'd said wistfully.

"Things can never be the way they were," she'd told him. "I'm not the same person I was, and I don't feel the same about you." Or about herself. She'd learned so much in these months on her own—knowledge that wouldn't allow her to return to the role of his perfect accessory again.

"That was a mean trick to play," Claire protested.

"*I* think it was smart," Steve said. "Do you want more children?"

"I wouldn't mind, but if that's not in the cards, I'm happy with the one I have." She smiled down at the baby sleeping beside her on the sofa.

"If you want more, I hope you meet a good man and have a chance to have them," Steve said. "You're a good mother."

His praise warmed her. She'd tried her best with Steve and his siblings, but she'd been flying blind, young and ignorant of what it took to be a parent. Her main goal had been to do a better job than her own mother had done.

"I'd be scared, raising a baby on my own," Claire said. "It's such a big responsibility."

"Women do it all the time," Steve said.

"Men, too," Derek added.

Claire made a face. "Well, yes, but my point is, with two people it's bound to be easier. Daddy might not be the greatest father in the world, but at least he was *there.* He paid the bills and went through the motions, if only because he knew how much it annoyed Mom to see him at our school plays and basketball games with his younger, pretty wife."

"I thought he attended those evenings because I nagged him about them," Diana said.

"I'm sure that had something to do with it," Steve said.

"I think one of the reasons Daddy didn't do more with us was because after they were married, Diana just stepped in and took over anything having to do with us kids," Claire said. "You didn't even give him a chance."

This view of her actions stunned Diana. "He didn't need my permission to be involved in his children's lives," Diana said. "Since when did your father need permission from anyone to do anything? He's spent a lifetime giving orders to others."

"Except when it came to us kids. You intimidated him. You were so sure you knew what was right for us that he let you take over."

Diana tried not to show how much this revelation hurt. She glanced at Steve. "Is that how you see it?"

He looked uncomfortable. "I think it was easier for him to take a back seat once you came along."

"I never meant to shut him out of your lives," she protested.

"Don't worry about it," Steve said. "If he'd really wanted to be there for us, nothing you did or said would have mattered."

"I suppose you're right," she said. But the revelation that she'd run roughshod over any feeble parenting attempts Richard had made cut deep. She'd given in to him on every other aspect of their lives—where to go on vacation, what kind of car they'd drive, even how to decorate their house. She hadn't even realized she'd asserted herself when it came to the children, though she could see now that this had been one area where she'd felt strongly enough to not even give him a chance to intimidate her.

The beginning of the end for their marriage had come

when the children were all grown and gone. She'd felt stymied once she no longer had a single area of independence. Was it possible one of the reasons Richard had objected so strongly to her pregnancy was a fear that she would once more take over and exclude him from playing a relevant role in his child's life? Did he see her as incapable of having a good relationship *and* being a good parent at the same time?

Was he right?

She felt sick with guilt, and had to force a smile when Eric and Micah returned to the room and the little boy came over to look at the baby. It made her wonder when else she had been sure she was right, when in fact, she was so wrong.

## CHAPTER FIFTEEN

CANDACE WAS SO PLEASED when Jason dropped his custody suit that she suggested he arrange to talk to Kinsey on Wednesdays *and* Saturdays. Kinsey was thrilled with the video camera and came to the computer with school papers, toys and pictures to share with her father. Now that he'd grown accustomed to his daughter's new haircut and clothes, he was doubly grateful to Graham for suggesting the cameras. Despite the distance between them, he felt closer to Kinsey than ever.

One crisis behind him, Jason wondered if he should give more serious consideration to some of Graham's other advice. Dating, for instance. Being with Diana had revealed a loneliness he hadn't been willing to acknowledge before. Maybe it was time he tried to find someone more suitable. He wasn't ready for marriage, but a pleasant companion to share occasional meals and long evenings with would be a welcome change from the endless, silent nights he faced now.

Beverly Polis was the most likely candidate. He decided he'd ask her out after the board meeting at the end of the week. The school's board of directors was coming to inspect the new playscape, which was almost complete. Though Jason hadn't heard a word from Diana, he assumed she'd been in contact with the builder. The structures still needed painting; they were waiting on a shipment of new, more subdued paint colors Jason had requested.

He thought the paint had arrived when Evie informed him that a truck had shown up with a new shipment for the playground. "Just tell them to stack the buckets against the wall," he said. "The contractor will take care of everything."

"Stack what against the wall?" Evie asked.

"The buckets of paint," he said. "For the playscape."

"This isn't paint," she said.

"What is it?"

"I'm not sure. Maybe you'd better come take a look."

He followed her out the side door and around to the playground. A large truck was backed up to the gate and two burly men were unloading half a dozen large packing crates. "What is all this?" Jason asked, hurrying to them.

One of the men stopped and pulled a packing manifest from his back pocket. "Are you Jason Benton?" he asked.

"Yes."

"Sign here." The man shoved the paper at Jason, handed him a pen and indicated a line at the bottom of the page.

"But what is it?" Jason studied the manifest. "'Deluxe jungle gym,'" he read.

"It's a deluxe jungle gym," the man said. He stuffed

the signed paper back into his pocket. "Looks like some assembly is required." He laughed at his own joke and dragged a third box out of the back of the truck.

Graham joined Jason and Evie near the stack of boxes. "What's all this?" he asked.

"A jungle gym," Evie said. "Or pieces of one, anyway."

"I didn't know the plans called for a jungle gym," Graham said.

"They don't." Jason felt light-headed, confusion and happiness battling for the upper hand. "Somebody get me something to open these boxes."

Evie left and returned a moment later with a large pair of scissors. Jason and Graham attacked the first box, stabbing and tearing until the cardboard and a layer of plastic sheeting were torn away to reveal the vinyl-coated metal curves and arches of what was clearly part of a classic jungle gym.

"Oh, my," Evie said. "It's very…bright."

Jason nodded. "It is." The structure was bright purple and yellow.

"What are you grinning about?" Graham asked. "I thought you didn't like bright colors."

Jason hadn't even realized he was grinning, but he couldn't stop himself. "No, purple and yellow is perfect," he said. He looked around the yard. "Where are the contractors?"

"They can't do anything else until the paint gets here," Evie said.

"Call them up and let them know they need to assemble this jungle gym," he said. "And have them talk to me about the paint."

DIANA DIDN'T KNOW whether to be puzzled or annoyed by the message Jason's secretary delivered to her: "Mr. Benton says you absolutely must be at the school Friday afternoon when the board of directors comes to inspect the playscape. They need you here to answer questions."

She'd hoped to hear from Jason after she sent the jungle gym—hoped he'd see the addition to the playground as a peace offering, her attempt to admit she wasn't always right. To receive this formal message, delivered in the form of an order, rankled. But it wasn't a request she could refuse. "Of course I'll be there," she said. "I'll be happy to answer any questions the board might have."

With luck, she'd avoid being alone with Jason, or speaking to him any more than necessary.

She arrived at the school Friday afternoon scarcely five minutes before the time Jason's secretary had given her. She unloaded Leah's carrier, then, instead of making her way through the school, walked around the side toward the playscape.

She stopped at the edge of the fenced yard to admire the finished product. The trio of tree trunks rose tall, their branches spreading out over the tree house, swings, slides and climbing wall. The jungle gym crouched in the shade of the branches, like some wildly colored forest growth—a bit discordant, but not entirely out of place.

Only then did she realize *why* the jungle gym fit in so well. Instead of the subdued greens and browns she'd reluctantly agreed on for the playscape's paint job, the trees and their various attachments were adorned in bright purple, blue and yellow, with touches of vibrant green. The effect was wild and colorful, the opposite of blending into the background, as Jason had wished.

She was still pondering the meaning of this when he emerged from the school and came toward her. "What do you think?" he asked.

"It's gorgeous," she said. "Exactly as I pictured it. But the colors?"

"If you could give in on the jungle gym, I knew I could compromise on the colors." He stopped beside her and faced the playscape. "You were right. It should be bright and fun. I'm man enough to admit I was wrong."

"And I'm woman enough to admit I was wrong, too." About a lot of things, but now was not the time or place to bare her soul. "Where are the board members?" she asked.

"They won't be arriving for another half hour or so."

"But your secretary told me to be here at two-thirty."

"She did? I'm sorry, she must have gotten the time wrong."

Leah began to fuss. Diana rocked the carrier. She'd hoped to get this meeting over with before time for the baby's next feeding, but apparently Leah had other ideas.

"If you want to wait in my office, you're welcome," Jason said.

"Yes, that would be a good idea," she said.

Leah continued to cry all the way to his office. "I think she's hungry," Diana said. "Could I nurse her for a few minutes?"

"Of course. I'll leave you alone in here. No one will bother you."

Before she could ask him to stay, he stepped out of the room, shutting the door behind him.

While Leah nursed, Diana looked around the office. Her drawings for the playscape were tacked to the wall, along with new pictures of Kinsey, the kind that might be taken with a video camera and printed from the Internet. The girl showed a gap-toothed grin and waved at the camera. In another shot, she was blowing kisses. Diana hoped she'd have the opportunity to meet Jason's daughter one day.

Leah had finished nursing and was almost asleep when a gentle tapping sounded on the door. "Diana?" Jason asked. "The contractor needs you on the playground."

"Come in. I'm almost done here." She finished buttoning her blouse and checked Leah's diaper. Dry so far.

"Sorry to disturb you," he said. "There's some papers he needs signed, or something."

She started to fit the sleeping child back into her carrier, but Jason stopped her. "I can look after her for you," he said. "I don't mind."

"Oh. Okay." She handed over the baby. He took her

with none of the hesitation strangers sometimes evinced. "I'll be right back."

The contractor wanted her approval of some minor modifications he'd made to the structures, and her signature on the final inspection so that he could submit his invoice for payment. Diana agreed to the changes, signed the paperwork, then hurried back to Jason's office.

As she neared the open door she heard the low murmur of Jason's voice. "You're a good little girl, aren't you?" he said. "Such a sweetheart."

Diana stopped, then cautiously peeked around the door frame. Jason was standing by his desk, rocking Leah gently in his arms, smiling and talking to her in soothing tones. A knot rose in Diana's throat. At the same time one loosened in her heart. How could she not love this man? Why had it taken her so long to admit it?

She moved into the room, shutting the door behind her.

He looked up from the baby. "She and I have been having a little talk," he said.

"About what?" She stepped closer, until they were practically face-to-face, the baby between them.

"About how foolish grown-ups can be sometimes."

"Yes." She had been foolish. But she would make up for it now. "I'm sorry I sent you away, Jason," she said. "I was scared—afraid of making a mistake and being left again." Her parents and Richard had both abandoned her when she needed them, but Jason was not like them. She could see that now.

"I'm sorry, too," he said. "Sorry that I've been so stubborn about getting my own way. I guess trying to control things was my way of avoiding being hurt. You made me see how wrong I was."

She leaned against him and laid her head on his shoulder. "We have more in common than I realized at first," she said. "You thought staying in control would keep you safe, while I thought the answer was maintaining my independence at any cost. Now I see that relying on other people—and allowing them to rely on you—isn't a weakness, but a strength."

"And sometimes giving up control is the smart way to act." He shifted Leah to one arm and used the other to gather Diana close. "I love you," he said.

"Even though I don't make the bed or keep a neat house, and I have a hard time getting anywhere on time?" she asked.

"I love you in spite of those things—and because of them. They're part of who you are, just as my orderliness and fondness for schedules is part of me."

"We'll be good for each other," she said. "As long as we refrain from driving each other crazy."

"We'll keep practicing compromise until we're good at it," he said.

"I love you, Jason. I have for a long while now. It feels good to say it."

"Not as good as it feels to hear it."

They kissed, a kiss as sweet and magical as any she'd ever known. That's how the board of directors found them—with their arms around each other and the child, their lips sealing a promise of love neither ever intended to break.

*Celebrate 60 years of pure reading pleasure with Harlequin®!*

*Silhouette® Romantic Suspense is celebrating with the glamour-filled, adrenaline-charged series*
LOVE IN 60 SECONDS
*starting in April 2009.*

*Six stories that promise to bring the glitz of Las Vegas, the danger of revenge, the mystery of a missing diamond, family scandals and ripped-from-the-headlines intrigue. Get your heart racing as love happens in sixty seconds!*

*Enjoy a sneak peek of*
USA TODAY *bestselling author Marie Ferrarella's*
*THE HEIRESS'S 2-WEEK AFFAIR.*
*Available April 2009 from*
*Silhouette® Romantic Suspense.*

Eight years ago Matt Shaffer had vanished out of Natalie Rothchild's life, leaving behind a one-line note tucked under a pillow that had grown cold: *I'm sorry, but this just isn't going to work.*

That was it. No explanation, no real indication of remorse. The note had been as clinical and compassionless as an eviction notice, which, in effect, it had been, Natalie thought as she navigated through the morning traffic. Matt had written the note to evict her from his life.

She'd spent the next two weeks crying, breaking down without warning as she walked down the street, or as she sat staring at a meal she couldn't bring herself to eat.

Candace, she remembered with a bittersweet pang, had tried to get her to go clubbing in order to get her to forget about Matt.

She'd turned her twin down, but she did get her act together. If Matt didn't think enough of their relationship to try to contact her, to try to make her understand why he'd changed so radically from lover to stranger, then to hell with him. He was dead to her, she resolved. And he'd remained that way.

Until twenty minutes ago.

The adrenaline in her veins kept mounting.

Natalie focused on her driving. Vegas in the daylight wasn't nearly as alluring, as magical and glitzy as it was after dark. Like an aging woman best seen in soft lighting, Vegas's imperfections were all visible in the daylight. Natalie supposed that was why people like her sister didn't like to get up until noon. They lived for the night.

Except that Candace could no longer do that.

The thought brought a fresh, sharp ache with it.

"Dammit, Candy, what a waste," Natalie murmured under her breath.

She pulled up before the Janus casino. One of the three valets currently on duty came to life and made a beeline for her vehicle.

"Welcome to the Janus," the young attendant said cheerfully as he opened her door with a flourish.

"We'll see," she replied solemnly.

As he pulled away with her car, Natalie looked up at the casino's logo. Janus was the Roman god with two faces, one pointed toward the past, the other facing the future. It struck her as rather ironic, given what she was doing here, seeking out someone from her past in order to get answers so that the future could be settled.

The moment she entered the casino, the Vegas phenomena took hold. It was like stepping into a world where time did not matter or even make an appearance. There was only a sense of "now."

Because in Natalie's experience she'd discovered that bartenders knew the inner workings of any establishment they worked for better than anyone else, she made her way to the first bar she saw within the casino.

The bartender in attendance was a gregarious man in his early forties. He had a quick, sexy smile, which was probably one of the main reasons he'd been hired. His name tag identified him as Kevin.

Moving to her end of the bar, Kevin asked, "What'll it be, pretty lady?"

"Information." She saw a dubious look cross his brow. To counter that, she took out her badge. Granted she wasn't here in an official capacity, but Kevin didn't need to know that. "Were you on duty last night?"

Kevin began to wipe the gleaming black surface of the bar. "You mean, during the gala?"

"Yes."

The smile gracing his lips was a satisfied one. Last night had obviously been profitable for him, she judged. "I caught an extra shift."

She took out Candace's photograph and carefully placed it on the bar. "Did you happen to see this woman there?"

The bartender glanced at the picture. Mild interest turned to recognition. "You mean, Candace Rothchild? Yeah, she was here, as loud and brassy as always. But not for long," he added, looking rather disappointed. There was always a circus when Candace was around, Natalie thought. "She and the boss had at it and then he had our head of security escort her out."

She latched on to the first part of his statement. "They argued? About what?"

He shook his head. "Couldn't tell you. Too far away for anything but body language," he confessed.

"And the head of security?" she asked.

"He got her to leave."

She leaned in over the bar. "Tell me about him."

"Don't know much," the bartender admitted. "Just that his name's Matt Shaffer. Boss flew him in from L.A., where he was head of security for Montgomery Enterprises."

There was no avoiding it, she thought darkly. She was going to have to talk to Matt. The thought left her cold. "Do you know where I can find him right now?"

Kevin glanced at his watch. "He should be in his office. On the second floor, toward the rear." He gave her the numbers of the rooms where the monitors that kept watch over the casino guests as they tried their luck against the house were located.

Taking out a twenty, she placed it on the bar. "Thanks for your help."

Kevin slipped the bill into his vest pocket. "Anytime, lovely lady," he called after her. "Anytime."

She debated going up the stairs, then decided on the elevator. The car that took her up to the second floor was empty. Natalie stepped out of the elevator, looked around to get her bearings and then walked toward the rear of the floor.

"Into the Valley of Death rode the six hundred," she silently recited, digging deep for a line from a poem by Tennyson. Wrapping her hand around a brass handle, she opened one of the glass doors and walked in.

The woman whose desk was closest to the door looked up. "You can't come in here. This is a restricted area."

Natalie already had her ID in her hand and held it up. "I'm looking for Matt Shaffer," she told the woman.

God, even saying his name made her mouth go dry. She was supposed to be over him, to have moved on with her life. What happened?

The woman began to answer her. "He's—"

"Right here."

The deep voice came from behind her. Natalie felt every single nerve ending go on tactical alert at the same moment that all the hairs at the back of her neck stood up. Eight years had passed, but she would have recognized his voice anywhere.

\* \* \* \* \*

*Why did Matt Shaffer leave heiress-turned-cop*
*Natalie Rothchild?*
*What does he know about the death of Natalie's*
*twin sister?*
*Come and meet these two reunited lovers and learn*
*the secrets of the Rothchild family in*
*THE HEIRESS'S 2-WEEK AFFAIR*
*by USA TODAY bestselling author*
*Marie Ferrarella.*
*The first book in Silhouette® Romantic Suspense's*
*wildly romantic new continuity,*
*LOVE IN 60 SECONDS!*
*Available April 2009.*

# CELEBRATE
# 60 YEARS
## OF PURE READING PLEASURE
## WITH HARLEQUIN®!

## Look for Silhouette®
## Romantic Suspense in April!

# *Love In 60 Seconds*
### Bright lights. Big city. Hearts in overdrive.

Silhouette® Romantic Suspense is celebrating
Harlequin's 60th Anniversary with six stories that
promise to bring readers the glitz of Las Vegas,
the danger of revenge, the mystery of a missing
diamond, and family scandals.

---

**Look for the first title, *The Heiress's 2-Week Affair*
by *USA TODAY* bestselling author
Marie Ferrarella, on sale in April!**

| | |
|---|---|
| *His 7-Day Fiancée* by **Gail Barrett** | May |
| *The 9-Month Bodyguard* by **Cindy Dees** | June |
| *Prince Charming for 1 Night* by **Nina Bruhns** | July |
| *Her 24-Hour Protector* by **Loreth Anne White** | August |
| *5 minutes to Marriage* by **Carla Cassidy** | September |

---

# REQUEST YOUR FREE BOOKS!

## 2 FREE NOVELS PLUS 2 FREE GIFTS!

HARLEQUIN®

*Super Romance*®

### Exciting, emotional, unexpected!

# HARLEQUIN

## *Super Romance*

# COMING NEXT MONTH

## Available April 14, 2009

**#1554 HOME AT LAST • Margaret Watson**
*The McInnes Triplets*
Fiona McInnes finally has the life in the Big Apple she'd always wanted. But when her father dies, she's forced to return home to help settle his estate. Now nothing's going as planned—including falling back in love with the man whose heart she shattered.

**#1555 A LETTER FOR ANNIE • Laura Abbot**
*Going Back*
Kyle Becker is over any feelings he had for Annie Greer. Then she returns to town, and suddenly he's experiencing those emotions again. But before he and Annie can share a future, Kyle must keep a promise to deliver a letter that could make her leave.

**#1556 A NOT-SO-PERFECT PAST • Beth Andrews**
Ex-con Dillon Ward has no illusions about who he is. Neither does his alluring landlord. But Nina Carlson needs him to repair her wrecked bakery—like, *yesterday*. And if there's one thing this struggling single mom knows, it's that nobody's perfect

**#1557 THE MISTAKE SHE MADE • Linda Style**
Tori Amhearst can't keep her identity secret much longer. Ever since she brought Lincoln Crusoe home after an accident took away his memory, she's loved him on borrowed time. Because once Linc knows who she really is, she'll lose him forever.

**#1558 SOMEONE LIKE HER • Janice Kay Johnson**
Adrian Rutledge comes to Middleton expecting to find his estranged mother. He does expect to find Lucy Peterson or a community that feels like home. Yet he gets this and more. Could it be that Lucy—and this town—is the family he's dreamed of?

**#1559 THE HOUSE OF SECRETS • Elizabeth Blackwell**
*Everlasting Love*
As soon as Alissa Franklin sees the old house, she knows it will be hers. With the help of handyman Danny—who has secrets of his own—she uncovers the truth about the original owners. But can a hundred-year-old romance inspire her to take a chance on love today?